March 1995

ARADUS

For Sis. Stirnemann —
For this sick day — this is a heartwarming story with a different twist! The lady who wrote this I know well — and it reflects her spirit! (It goes along with the book I'm reading — Beauty and the Beast —)

Love you!

Happy Reading

ARADUS

A Biblical Novel
By Carol Dixon

Aradus
by Carol Dixon

©1994 Word Aflame Press
Hazelwood, MO 63042-2299

Cover Design by Tim Agnew

The Scripture quotations in this book are from *The Holy Bible, New King James Version,* Copyright 1982, by Thomas Nelson, Inc.

All rights reserved. No portion of this publication may be reproduced, stored in an electronic system or transmitted in any form or by any means, electronic, mechanical, photocopy, recording, or otherwise, without the prior permission of Word Aflame Press. Brief quotations may be used in literary reviews.

Printed in United States of America.

Printed by

Library of Congress Cataloging-in-Publication Data

Dixon, Carol.
    Aradus / by Carol Dixon.
      p. cm.
    ISBN 1-56722-019-3
     1. Centurion at the Crucifixion (Biblical figure)—Fiction.
2. Bible. N.T.—History of Biblical events—Fiction. 3. Jesus Christ—Crucifixion—Fiction. I. Title
PS3554.I868A89 1994
813' .54—dc20   93-49597
                                                        CIP

DEDICATION

*This novel is lovingly dedicated to
my husband, Steve,
who has always believed in my dreams.*

CHAPTER ONE

*H*e was ugly. It was the first thing one noticed, the first impression he made wherever he went. It wasn't just common, rough features but a horrible disfigurement that repelled everyone he met.

Jewish mothers would use him to frighten their mischievous children. "Better behave," they'd say, "or that hideous Roman centurion will come and take you away!"

Aradus Marcus had seen disgust in too many eyes. It was a hard thing to be the object of so much aversion. The pain of it had eaten at him until his heart was as scarred and calloused as his face.

Stationed at Jerusalem, Aradus was now on leave. He was making his way towards Capernaum to visit an uncle. A centurion like himself, his uncle was a sophisticated man with many ideas similar to his own.

The hot sun beat down on him, but he would not remove his heavy, ornate helmet. He and his horse were nearing a small village, and he would soon be among people again. His helmet gave him a sense of comfort as it hid nearly all of his face.

This must be Nazareth, he told himself. As he looked over the village, backed by gentle hills and faced by a smooth plain of green, he felt a peace come over him.

What was it like to grow up in such a town? How different it was from the noise and excitement of Rome. What a simple life it would be, with no greater responsibilities than caring for a wife and family. Roman soldiers were not allowed to marry until their military careers were over. It made for a lonely life.

Still Aradus could not really see himself there. What would I do in such a place, he asked himself, be a carpenter? He actually laughed out loud at the thought, a rare thing for him.

An answering giggle caused his head to spin around.

A large rock by the road was his only company. Curious, Aradus reined in his mount and waited, his right hand moving to his scabbard. Presently, a small imp of a boy made his way around the slab of stone.

Aradus made no greeting. It was his habit to let others speak first while he fixed them with an intimidating stare. It was a mannerism that had served him well.

The boy looked down at his feet for a moment, as if properly cowed. Then he looked boldly up at Aradus and giggled again. With perfect ease, he made a small bow and smiled broadly at the Roman.

"Peace be with you, sir," he said in a high, clear voice.

Aradus was surprised. It had been a long time since someone had smiled at him.

He studied the boy before him. The lad was slight. His feet were bare, but his thin body was clothed in a clean and well-made tunic. His hair was black and curly. It fell down into a pair of large brown eyes. Aradus grimaced as he noted the boy's nose. It promised to be big even if the rest of him never grew.

Aradus deigned to nod at the boy. He admired the boy's composure. How calm he stood while a mounted Roman soldier loomed over him.

"Greetings, little man," Aradus finally said.

The boy's smile threatened to split his face. Making another small bow, he answered, "Greetings, sir. Will you be needing a place for the night? My father has the finest inn." He paused, then added, "No bugs. Not a single bug in the place!"

"No bugs?" Aradus intoned with gruff suspicion. The boy amused him, but he chose not to show it.

The boy made a sound for emphasis, then stated enthusiastically, "They wouldn't dare show their face with my mother around."

Aradus allowed a grin to play with his mouth, then suppressed it. "I'll admit, boy, you look clean enough for your kind. But I'll be riding through and have no need for lodging."

The boy drooped a little in disappointment.

A sudden rumble in his stomach reminded Aradus that he hadn't eaten in hours. "This fearsome mother of yours, can she cook?"

With renewed vigor the child pumped his head up and down in the affirmative. "Oh yes! The very best—"

Aradus held up a hand for silence. "Very well. You have a name?"

"Yes sir! Guni."

"Then, Guni, run ahead and tell your mother to fix me a meal. Real hot food now, nothing stale or moldy." He gave Guni a fierce look, "I will hold you personally responsible, Guni, if I find a bug in my bowl!"

Guni only laughed and ran off towards the village.

Aradus sighed and fingered his horse's mane. "Croesus,

either that boy is too dense to be afraid of me, or he is braver than most of the men I have seen in this spineless country."

He rode slowly, thinking of the boy. His opinion of the Jews could not have been much lower. Since his stay in Judea, so many had groveled before him, either in fear or to gain his favor. Aradus felt any non-Roman to be inferior; even the Greeks he judged as only intellectual servants of Rome. The Jews, though, he held in deepest contempt.

He had often seen the Jews at their worst. Angry, afraid, frustrated at their domination by the Romans, they had never presented a pleasing face to him. He didn't seek to understand them; he simply loathed them.

As Aradus approached, he saw that Nazareth was a prettier town than many he had seen in Palestine. It was in a secluded valley in lower Galilee, a little north of the great plain of Esdraelon. A small hill rose up in the northwest part of the valley, with ravines cut on its east slope. On that slope rested the village of Nazareth.

It was a small place, a good two months' journey from Rome. The tetrarch Antipas rarely gave it a thought, as long as the taxes kept rolling in and the people behaved themselves.

Its buildings were made of white limestone from the investing hills. The houses were situated among fig trees, olive trees, and some cypress. Down below in the valley were gardens surrounded by hedges of prickly pear. In the midst of the gardens was a large enclosed fountain. Many women were gathered there getting water for their households. As Aradus drew near he could see they were mainly collecting gossip.

The laughter and lively banter at the fountain dried up as soon as the women saw the soldier riding towards them. They glanced nervously at each other as he rode up. One addled young girl let her heavy earthen jug slip from her fingers. The loud crash it made as it hit a stone and shattered caused them all to jump.

Even Aradus became uneasy. He had fought blue-painted Britons in their own woods, and he had chased Gauls through swampy marshes, but there was something unnerving in facing a knot of women. Especially since so many of them were young and possessed dark, liquid eyes.

"There's an inn near here." It came out harsh, like a command, yet Aradus had only meant to ask a question.

Two of the women looked at each other with trepidation. After a moment the older of the pair came forward. "Yes, my husband and I own the inn. Is there a problem?"

"No, no problem. I . . . uh, thought to get a meal and fodder for my horse."

The woman sighed. She had feared that at the least the empire was going to garrison a troop of soldiers at her inn, or perhaps announce another crippling tax. A meal she could handle. She offered a small prayer of thanks to Jehovah, then gave a shy smile to the Roman.

"There it is," she said, pointing up the hill to a building. "My daughter and I must finish getting water, then we will be there presently."

Aradus nodded and quickly moved away. Since Rome banned marriage for its soldiers, Aradus had resolved to have as little to do with women as possible. An errant breeze wafted the sweet ointment the women wore, causing Aradus to feel his loss. He shook his head and rode a little faster, quickly ascending the knoll of the hill.

As Roman soldiers were rarely seen there, Aradus attracted a great deal of attention. His scarlet cape announced he was not just a soldier, but a centurion, a seasoned warrior in command of nearly a hundred men. The more knowledgeable among the people could see that Aradus was a decorated hero. A jeweled medallion on his scabbard caught the sunlight and glittered brightly. Such medallions were only given to the most deserving.

His presence troubled the people, who thought he could only be bringing more hardship. Families gathered in doorways as he passed, watching in silence. If he happened to glance their way, they would drop their gaze, hoping to hide the hatred in their eyes.

He was not troubled by such a reception. Of course they hated him. They were the vanquished and he was of the victor nation. He cared nothing for their regard, only their compliance.

Still, there was one person in Nazareth who was glad to see him. Guni ran out of an alleyway, smiling and waving. "Over here!" he called exuberantly, "I haven't seen Mother, but my father had one of the girls start your meal. It's nearly ready."

"Your mother was at the well. She's coming," Aradus said shortly as he dismounted.

Guni led him through an archway that opened into a small courtyard. There was a well in the center, with a few rooms and stalls along the sides of the square. It was perhaps the smallest inn Aradus had yet seen. Still, considering how rare it was to be able to purchase a hot meal in this province, he felt fortunate.

A short, thin man appeared at the opposite archway. He hesitated, clasping his hands in a nervous fashion, and then began to walk slowly towards them. The man had a mass of dark curls that could stand a good trim. His squinting brown eyes were overwhelmed by an immense nose that bore a strong resemblance to Guni's.

He laid a protective hand on Guni's shoulder as he looked

up at Aradus. "Good day, centurion. My son tells us you would like food for yourself and your horse."

From habit, Aradus stared at the man in silence. Then from the corner of his eye he could see Guni's beaming face. The boy was watching his father with obvious pride.

Aradus allowed his harsh features to soften slightly. "Yes, a hot meal for myself and fodder for the horse," he said, then after a long pause, "please."

The little man relaxed a bit. Perhaps we will survive this, he thought to himself.

A lanky boy with the same family features appeared and led the horse to a stall. The father directed Aradus into yet another archway while Guni ran to collect his friends.

It was a very clean room Aradus was brought to. He saw that the mother and daughter were there, busy with the last preparations. A wonderful odor of cooking food filled the room.

He sat where he was shown and removed his heavy helmet. The women stared at him for a moment, then hurriedly looked away. Aradus paid no heed. He knew too well what he looked like. Twenty years in the Roman army had taken its toll.

As the women placed the food in front of him, they steadfastly kept their eyes down, either from shyness or to keep from staring. It gave him ample opportunity to regard them. The mother was quite a bit taller then her husband. She was also bigger boned with a broad, pleasant face. The daughter was about thirteen. As he studied the girl, he decided she had better cook well and smile often. No man would grow lovesick from that face.

Guni appeared again with an assortment of friends. As they began to crowd into the doorway his mother started to shoo them away.

"Let the boy stay," Aradus heard himself say. "He amuses me."

With new self-importance, Guni left his friends at the door. He sat down with a thud, across from the Roman. He had not seen Aradus before without his helmet. He stared intently, watching every movement of Aradus's scarred visage.

The parents were in agony, fearful that Guni would make some offending remark. They tried in vain to get the boy's attention, but his eyes were riveted to the Roman's face.

Aradus ate in seeming oblivion to the boy's rudeness. He gave all his attention to the well-deserving fish and lentils. In silence he ate his pomegranates and figs. Then as he quaffed the last of the sweet wine, he looked Guni squarely in the eye. "All right, boy, ask me."

The father felt a lurching in his stomach.

"That big dent in your forehead, how did it happen?"

"A barbarian from Briton clubbed me."

So entranced was Guni that he didn't realize what he said next. "Did you live?"

Delighted, Aradus actually laughed out loud. "Yes, but the Briton didn't. However I was senseless for three days. When I came to myself I was lying across my horse."

"The scar that runs from your eye to your ear. How did it happen?"

"The Gauls are fair archers. I had moved my head just as the arrow went by."

"How fortunate you were!"

"Yes, but the man behind me was most unlucky."

The parents were desperate to turn the conversation. Thankfully, Guni became quiet, though he still stared at Aradus's ruined face. Suddenly his eyes got even bigger. "Excuse me!" he yelped, as he jumped from the table and dashed through the doorway.

Surprised and relieved, the father timidly smiled at Aradus. "Please forgive Guni. He's a good boy but very impetuous."

"There is nothing to forgive. He speaks his mind; I like that."

Rising, Aradus pulled a leather pouch from within his belt. He took out a few coins that were nearly three times the meal's worth. He had really enjoyed talking to the boy.

The father shook his head as Aradus tried to pay him. "No, that is too much."

"Take it. The boy amuses me. I would have paid twice this just to hear him." He paused, then added, "Besides, there were no bugs. Surely I must pay extra for that."

The women gave a gasp of indignation that the father silenced with a glance. He meekly allowed the Roman to put the coins in his hand. When Aradus left, the father slumped into a chair, his legs too weak to hold him any longer.

As Aradus returned the concealing helmet to his head, he looked about for a glimpse of the boy. Even after he retrieved his horse and left the courtyard, the boy did not appear.

Aradus was surprised to find he was disappointed at not saying goodbye to the child. He had never noticed children before.

He had mounted Croesus and nearly left the village, when the sound of running feet caused him to turn his head.

Guni was racing towards him, leading a band of young boys. "Wait, wait!" Guni stopped upon reaching him. He held his hands to his chest as he gasped for air.

"Get your breath, boy, I'll wait."

"I . . . I . . . wanted to help you . . . but He's gone."

Aradus was silent, waiting for the boy to explain himself.

"You see, I know a man who can heal you."

"Heal me? I'm not sick."

"No. Heal your face. He can fix your awful face."

Aradus was torn between being amused or offended. Looking at Guni's earnest expression, he decided to laugh. "My face troubles you, eh? But I am so used to it, I'm not sure I want it fixed."

Guni seemed stung by the Roman's laughter. His friends joined in with giggles and taunts, increasing his dismay.

"Don't mind them," Guni said with the last of his dignity. "They don't believe in Jesus."

"Jesus? So He is the physician. He'd need to be a sorcerer to mend this poor face," Aradus said gently.

"He is a sorcerer," a boy yelled.

"Sorcerer? He's a devil!" shouted another.

Tears of anger began to burn Guni's eyes. He feared he was going to cry in front of his new friend. Sensing the boy's dilemma, Aradus glared at the jeering boys, who subsided instantly.

"Don't mind them," Guni said, a small lip quivering. "They only repeat what their fathers say. We've known Him all our lives. He's only been kind and good to us."

"Where is He now?"

"He's gone to Capernaum."

"That is where I am going, Guni. If I see Him I will remove my helmet and let Him work His magic on my face."

It was the wrong thing to say. Guni resented being patronized in front of his friends. He was hurt that the Roman would not take him seriously. "It is not magic! Surely you do not want to be that ugly all your life!"

The other boys gasped in horror, certain the awful soldier would now run their friend through with his sword.

Strangely, he only laughed again. It occurred to Aradus he had laughed more in one day than he had in weeks. He looked down on the fuming Guni and saluted. "Son, you should have been a Roman."

With that he turned his horse around and rode away.

CHAPTER TWO

*A*radus was still smiling two miles down the road. He had not expected to find so much spirit in all of Palestine, let alone in the person of such a small boy.

The Roman wondered that the boy was so concerned over his face. His ugly injuries had taken a heavy toll on his life, but why should that bother the boy?

As an officer in an occupied country, there were very few people who would dare mention his face to him. Just as scarce were the highly polished bronze mirrors that could remind him of his man-made deformities.

In fact, as much as he hated to admit it, his posting in Jerusalem had been a blessing in disguise. In this obscure exile he was safe from the pity of former acquaintances, safe from the looks of horror that those who had once admired his looks would give him.

As Aradus thought upon these things, his characteristic frown returned. Yes, it had been quite a while since he had really dwelt on his injuries and all they had cost him.

No one who presently knew him could ever imagine Aradus as a handsome young man with an engaging manner, a man who smiled often and laughed loudly. Despite his fierceness in battle, he had been a kind man and an understanding commander—once.

Now he was vastly different. Cold and aloof, he gave the men under him no quarter. He demanded the same rigorous obedience from them that he gave to his superiors. If he had a heart, which many doubted, he kept it carefully guarded. In truth, it had more scars than his face.

Aradus rode for hours, determined to reach Capernaum by nightfall. He was glad when the road finally took him into the Plain of Gennesaret. There was a freshness in the air that told him he would soon be seeing the Sea of Galilee. After that, it wouldn't be long before he reached the city.

The plain was formed by a recession of the hills from the shore just north of Magdala and measured about three miles by one and a half. It was watered by a fountain known as Capharnaum. It made an ideal place for the growth of walnut, palm, and fig trees. Bright red poppies dotted the landscape, lining the road he traveled.

Aradus drank in the sight. He wondered that there could be such beauty and diversity in one place. In his more thoughtful moments, he had questioned how the world had come to be. He had read Lucretius, who had set forth his theory that creation was the result of atoms moving about in space. He hadn't understood it all, but he did agree with Lucretius that it was a waste for humans to pay homage to a religion in which gods created the earth.

Most of his fellow Romans would have easily explained this beautiful plan. The goddess Ceres kept it watered and fruitful. Aradus had little regard for such beliefs. In his harsh life, he had never found a reason to worship or give thanks to any god.

His stationing in Judea had confirmed his disbelief. Never had he met a more religious people than the Jews. Not only were they devout, but they gave all their worship to just one God. Where did it get them? They were under the complete domination of a foreign power. Surely if such a God existed He would be working on their behalf. He had heard the tales of a coming Messiah and deliverance for the Jews, but he considered them vain stories, meant to placate and comfort oppressed people.

No, it was far better to trust in yourself, Aradus reasoned. Depend on no one, care for no one. Carve out a life for yourself and be prepared to die bravely.

Such were his thoughts as he saw his road edging toward the Sea of Galilee. A cool breeze came up to him. He removed his helmet, the better to feel the air. It blew harder then, caressing the tired rider and his horse.

He reined his horse to a halt and gazed out over the lake. The sun seemed large and liquid as it prepared to set for the evening. The sky was filled with impossible shades of purple, red, and ocher.

The sea reflected these colors, then broke them into bits of refracted light, like shattered glass on an azure floor.

He found himself wishing there was a God to thank for such a sight. "Lucretius, how could your atoms do all this by themselves?" he mused aloud. Receiving no answer from the wind and sea, he continued on towards Capernaum.

CHAPTER THREE

As the sky had darkened, Aradus was able to make out small pinpoints of light down the road. A large smile worked its way across his face. Capernaum at last. If he had not been so mindful of his weary horse, he would have forced it into a gallop.

For all his independence, Aradus longed to see his uncle. Aradus's bitter nature had made him a loner. He barely deigned to speak to the men under him, he didn't trust the centurions of equal rank, nor would he unbend to his superiors. He was starved for conversation. He would be able to talk with his uncle, a centurion like himself. Yes, he told himself, talk long and freely, talk for hours of Rome and the world, but don't trust him, don't trust even your uncle.

Capernaum was a Roman military post, so Aradus was not surprised to see two soldiers walking towards him as he entered the town. The two men stopped to the left of his horse and saluted Aradus. He returned the salute, peering down at them through the twilight. Even in the dark, Aradus could tell their appearance was disheveled. The stench of strong, cheap wine attacked his nostrils. The men looked to be auxiliaries, hired soldiers the empire employed for its dirtier work. Not true Romans, but half-civilized foreign subjects.

The men shifted unhappily as Aradus held their gaze in silence. He noticed that the larger of the two men carried a small canvas sack under his arm. The sack moved in short, quick jerks. Aradus stared for a full minute longer, then finally spoke. "I trust you are both off duty?"

"Yes, centurion," they replied in unison.

They were off duty and not even his men. Still their sloppy form in public irritated him. Where was their pride?

"And the sack?" he asked gruffly.

The taller soldier opened his mouth, then shut it in confusion. His companion glanced nervously at him and began to speak.

"Yes sir, the sack. You see, the people here can be most generous. A family gave us this chicken as a gift."

"A gift?"

"Indeed sir, for some trivial thing . . . hardly worth mentioning."

Aradus was well aware how scarce fowl were in this province. He couldn't imagine a Jewish family giving up one voluntarily. "Strange, that such a grateful family would not even take the time to kill and dress this gift of yours."

The shorter man was ready with another glib excuse, but the sight of Aradus unsheathing his sword silenced him. With a deft movement the centurion reached down and hooked a piece of the bag on his sword. Tossing it into the air, he caught it again with his left hand.

"Surely soldiers of Rome should not be in debt to Jews," Aradus murmured with a dangerous softness. "Where does this grateful family live?"

While one soldier pointed, the other gave precise directions. The two men were sober enough to realize the thinly veiled rage coming from this strange officer. His anger confused them, and they were fearful lest they provoke him further.

Aradus studied them in the moonlight, intent upon memorizing their features. He was bound to come across them again in this tiny province. And good commander that he was, he would not forget such pettiness.

After what seemed like hours of agony, Aradus finally turned his head away in disgust. "You may go."

The men saluted and quickly walked away. Aradus watched as they hurried down the deserted street, wondering at himself. These men were really none of his concern, yet it angered him to see Roman soldiers act like looting barbarians. His pride in the empire was one of the few constants in his life. Shaking his head, he turned his horse down the street.

He stopped at the house the soldiers had pointed out. He could hear scuffling within. The crack of light that had shone under the door suddenly vanished. Unconcerned, Aradus dismounted and walked to the door. Using the heft of his dagger, he pounded loudly on the weathered wood. Even in the moonlight he could see the dents he was making in the door. "You do not want to keep me waiting in the street!" he said imperiously, barely raising his voice.

The light quickly reappeared under the door. Aradus grimaced.

The door opened to show an older man poorly dressed. Aradus looked passed him to a smoking lamp in the corner. He saw that the lamp was held by a young girl. The girl's face was swollen and tear stained. Something close to compassion rose within him, but he quickly dismissed it. Turning back to the man, he thrust the bobbing sack at him and asked harshly, "Is this thing yours?"

As the man looked at the bag a world of emotion crossed his face. Relief and curiosity were quickly replaced by fear. He was uncertain whether to claim it.

"Here, take it." Aradus pushed it at him.

"I . . . I don't understand," the man stammered.

"The empire conquers nations; it does not stoop to pilfering . . . chickens."

A gruesome thought occurred to the centurion as he looked back to the young girl cowering in the corner. "Nothing else was taken?"

The man looked puzzled for a moment, then understanding broke upon his face with a blush. "Oh! No, no. My daughter cried because the chicken was a pet."

How absurd, Aradus thought, but kept the sentiment to himself. Shrugging his large shoulders, he turned to go.

"Sir?" the old man spoke timidly.

"Yes."

"Indeed I do thank you. I am most grateful . . ."

"Yes?" As Aradus turned back he saw the old man's watery eyes were bright and alert, brimming with curiosity. If he hadn't been Jewish, Aradus would have thought him a scholar.

The man's height forced him to crane his neck back as he looked up at the Roman's face. His reddish brows were drawn together in confusion. "I appreciate your returning our pet, but I don't understand it."

"I wouldn't expect you to!" was the gruff reply.

Irritated, Aradus mounted his horse and rode down the street. It nettled him that the Jew would think a Roman incapable of morals or justice.

His thoughts were as dark as the streets he rode through. For the first time he had been touched by the contempt the

Jews held for the Romans. For the first time, he wondered if some of that contempt could be deserved. Drunken soldiers stealing family pets. Where was the glory of Rome in that? His brooding was interrupted by a welcome sight. Across from the lane he had entered, he saw where the garrison was posted. Situated on a bluff, overlooking the lake, he could see the well-made walls that contained Capernaum's military post.

He was readily admitted by the guards and shown to a large whitewashed building left of the barracks. Ornamental cypress trees were stationed at the corners of the building. A carefully raked path of gravel led to a polished wooden door set in the wall. Aradus smiled to himself. Yes, this was his uncle's quarters as surely as if he had painted his name on the walls.

Aradus dismounted and went to the door. With a vastly different manner of knocking than he had used earlier, he rapped respectfully on the polished wood. The shuffling sound of sandals on stone told him someone was coming.

The heavy door opened inward to reveal a youth of about fourteen. He was nearly as tall as Aradus but much thinner. His blue eyes and blond hair were a novelty. The ring in his ear showed him to be a slave, probably from some northern holding.

The youth greeted him shyly, his strange accent confirming Aradus's guess.

Before Aradus could respond the boy bowed clumsily and ushered him inside. The boy was at an awkward age but was already showing the signs of a good servant. Surely he was being well treated.

Another slave appeared, this one a middle-aged man. He was respectful but poised. "Sir, may I stable your horse?" he asked quietly.

Aradus gave him only a nod, then looked past him down the hall. The youth took the cue and began to lead him to a well-lit room in the back.

The room itself was large and plainly made, but it was filled with the choicest of furnishings. As Aradus's eyes adjusted to the bright light supplied by the many braziers, he saw his uncle reclining on a couch in the corner. The older man was reading a large scroll that he held in his hands. So absorbed was he, that he hadn't noticed the two men entering.

Except for the graying hair, Aradus's uncle had changed little in the years since he had last seen him. Still a very thin man, his height made him appear even thinner. He possessed a pair of black, piercing eyes that could bore a hole through any recalcitrant soldier. Those eyes were now focused on the parchment as if they held the secrets of the universe.

The slave had to clear his throat twice before the man looked up. When he finally glanced towards the disturbing sound and saw his nephew standing before him, his face broke into a smile of pure delight.

"Aradus!" he cried, leaping up with the agility of a much younger man. He grasped his nephew by the shoulders and gave a hard, affectionate shake.

"Uncle Lyconides," Aradus smiled and grasped his uncle's arms, but felt constrained from showing much emotion in front of the slave.

Glancing at his nephew, then at the slave, Lyconides cocked an eyebrow. "Off with you, Avva," he said bluffly. "Go tell the cook my nephew has come." Smiling back at Aradus, he announced, "We shall dine shortly."

Avva walked out and the middle-aged man appeared again. He carried a large basin of water with a thick, heavy cloth slung across his shoulder. As he approached, Lyconides waved expansively towards the ornate couch he had just vacated. "Sit, Aradus. Sit. Drusus will wash the Judean dust off those big feet of yours."

Aradus sat down gladly. It was a relief to feel his weight supported by something more yielding than the back of his horse. He glanced down at the slave kneeling before him and wondered why this dignified man had been given the lowliest job in the household. His attention, though, was immediately reclaimed by his uncle.

"So, my stalwart soldier, will you not even remove your helmet?" Lyconides joked. "Do you always socialize in full armor? Come, let me see if my favorite brother still lives in your face."

With great reluctance Aradus removed the helmet and carefully laid it beside him on the couch. He busied himself with a strap so he wouldn't have to see the smile dying from his uncle's face.

After a few heartbeats, Aradus was ready to accept the shocked repugnance in his uncle's eyes. Yet when he looked up there was no repugnance to be found. Compassion welled in Lyconides's black eyes.

Both men were silent. They studied each other while they waited for the slave to finish the menial task of foot washing.

Drusus was soon done. He allowed himself a quick glance at the Roman's ruined face, then bowing he left the room.

Hoping to keep the conversation impersonal, Aradus nodded towards the doorway. "Uncle, such elegant slaves. Have you been kidnapping senators and forcing them into foot washing? Will I be tempted to bow to your cook?"

"Eh?" Lyconides was slow to regain his usual cheerful demeanor. "Oh, I see what you mean. No, Drusus is the father of the young boy who showed you in. He wants Avva to be well trained, so they're trading jobs for a few days."

"Concerned that his son would not be a proper slave?" The younger man was suddenly bitter. "How touching to find such parental ambition."

Lyconides was a study in surprise and guilt. His well-defined brows lifted high over his rounded eyes. He shrugged his shoulders and spread out the long fingers of his hands. "It is the way of things. The boy will always be a slave. He might as well be a good one."

"Uncle! Heavens, I was not reproaching you! What are these brute beasts to us?"

"Indeed . . ." Lyconides murmured as he looked towards the open doorway. He adjusted his snowy white tunic with an elegant hand and turned back to Aradus. "The years have been hard on you, my boy."

"I'd forgotten how long it had been since we last met. You've never seen my . . . 'war trophies.'"

"No. Your poor forehead. How did you survive such a blow?"

"Ah, you know what a hard head I have. Don't look so sad, Uncle. At least I'm behind this face and not in front of it. In fact, I am seldom even troubled by mirrors in this forsaken wasteland."

Without wishing it, his uncle's eyes darted to the wall behind his nephew. Turning, Aradus saw what his uncle was looking at, though he knew what it would be before he looked. There on the wall, half hidden by shadows, was a large, bronze mirror. Of course.

Aradus was tempted for a moment, then he turned to his uncle with a shrug.

Lyconides moved forward and picked up the scroll from the couch. His hands caressed the creamy parchment as he held it thoughtfully to his chest.

Before he could speak, Aradus continued. "Now, don't look so concerned. I have been told with great earnestness that I can be healed."

"Healed?"

"Yes. A little Jewish boy told me some friend of his has the power to 'cure' this face."

His uncle did not smile as he had expected. "His friend, what was his name?"

"Hmm. I don't recall . . . wait, Joseph?"

"Jesus?"

"Jesus! Yes that's it. But how could you know?"

CHAPTER FOUR

"*J*esus."

Lyconides walked to a nearby table. He carefully placed the scroll down before he continued speaking. "Yes, that is quite a common name around here."

"Well, this Jesus is anything but common. According to the little boy, He's capable of performing miracles. But then these Jews seem quite fond of magicians."

"True. The people, then, think Jesus is just a sorcerer?"

Aradus leaned to one side, making himself more comfortable. He was glad to have the conversation shift from himself. "What the people think, I wouldn't know. But a certain group of boys were quite divided on the subject. Not all of them were as fond of Jesus as little Guni."

"Really?"

"Yes. In fact, one boy stoutly declared him to be a devil!" Aradus grunted. "Tell me, have you ever met anyone as superstitious as these Jews?"

A movement from the doorway stopped Lyconides from answering. A red-faced Drusus was standing there. "Sirs," he announced, "the meal is ready."

Lyconides gave him a kind smile, then a nod. After the man left, he turned to his nephew and said quietly, "Drusus is a Jew. In fact, so are many in my household."

"Yes?" Aradus said absently, missing the hint. He was busy picking up the scroll from the table. He looked at it in surprise then turned to Lyconides. "This is Hebrew, Uncle. Can you read it?"

"Yes."

"I am impressed. That's no mean feat. So what great piece of culture is written here?"

Lyconides looked uncomfortable, then made a dismissive shrug of his shoulders. "I doubt it would interest you. Come, my boy, let's eat. I think I can tempt you with viands beyond your officer's mess."

Aradus rose from the couch. "My horse is probably eating better tonight than my men in Jerusalem."

As he followed his uncle through the lovely rooms, he noticed there was a complete lack of the usual art and statuary Lyconides was so fond of. It occurred to him there wasn't even a small statue of Mars, the god of war. Cynic though Aradus was, he had a tiny replica of Mars in his quarters. Just in case.

This lack seemed strange in someone as refined and cultured as Lyconides. Yet all questions left him as Aradus saw the sumptuous table his uncle had prepared for him. He had not seen such a variety of dishes since he had left Rome. Taking the couch pointed out to him, Aradus reclined and prepared to enjoy the dinner.

As good as the food was, the young centurion enjoyed the meal more for the treat of unreserved conversation he had with his uncle. Normally a quiet man, he found himself quite talkative in Lyconides's presence. "Listen to me!" he finally said, after the dishes had been cleared away. "I'm gossiping like some old crone at the village well. You will tire of me and wish me gone on the morrow!"

"Never. If anything I shall hide your horse to prevent your going at all."

Aradus stared into the bottom of his cup for a long moment, then raised his eyes to his uncle's. "It's been a while since I've been a welcomed guest in someone's home."

"Not a guest. You're family." Lyconides's voice was warm. "As close to a son as I'm likely to get."

Uncomfortable with such kindness, Aradus was quick to lighten his tone. "Now, now. You'll be able to retire soon and start a family. Remember old Titus Camillus? Got married at sixty? Last I heard he had fathered two sons, and all signs seem to indicate another one shortly."

Lyconides smiled and shook his head. He traced an idle pattern on the table with his finger for a moment, then began to speak softly, wistfully. "The empire is a hard taskmaster. Haven't you ever wondered what our lives would have been like if we'd been allowed to marry during our military careers?"

Aradus disliked any criticism of Rome. Shrugging his shoulders, he sat his cup down. "The empire must be hard, sir. That hardness makes us rulers instead of servants. We sit at tables such as this, while others scrape out our dirty plates."

As Lyconides studied his nephew he wondered at the man he had become. His harsh features were not just the results of his injuries. After a few hours in the younger man's presence he had already become used to the sight of his ruined face. It was his attitude, his spirit that he could not get used to.

"Of course," Lyconides said at last. "Pay me no heed. I

will blame the lateness of the hour for my grumblings. You must—"

He broke off as Avva reappeared with a fresh flagon of wine. Lyconides stared at him as he sat the small vessel on the table. "Avva, what's wrong with you?"

Aradus turned to look at the youth, surprised by his uncle's question. He could see now that the boy's face was very flushed. Not that he would have noticed it. Who regarded such things?

Before the boy could answer, Lyconides reached over and clasped his wrist. "Why you are burning with fever."

"No, sir, I'm fine."

"Nonsense. Tell Drusus to come here, then get yourself to bed."

Avva nodded glumly, then walked away. With concern, Lyconides watched him go.

"He's a fine young man. Never complains about anything."

"Oh?" Aradus murmured, trying to stifle a yawn and not succeeding very well.

"Yes, he's practically grown up under my roof. Took his first steps . . ." Lyconides trailed off as he saw his nephew's disinterest.

Drusus entered at that point, coming slowly to the table.

"Drusus, I've packed Avva off to bed. He seems to have quite a fever. Tell your wife she's free to use any medicines we might have."

Aradus wondered in silence as his uncle discussed with the boy's father the best treatments for fever. His concern seemed to equal that of a parent.

After Drusus left, Aradus commented, "You are good to your people, Uncle."

"Am I? I often wonder." Lyconides stood up abruptly in a

single graceful movement. The crisp linen of his tunic fell in soft folds around his slim form. "Come, you must be exhausted. Not to mention that I have duties in the morning."

Feeling suddenly boorish in comparison to his elegant uncle, Aradus hoped Lyconides was not sorry he'd invited him. Perhaps he should have written of his injuries, warning him of the face that would be staying with him.

As he followed his uncle, a wave of bitterness replaced his earlier good feelings. What had he been thinking? His uncle was an officer of high stature here; surely he wouldn't want some freak of a relative parading about the post. Aradus was suddenly thankful that he'd come at night and as always had his helmet on. He resolved to give his uncle as graceful an excuse as possible. Surely he could think of some plausible reason for leaving tomorrow, as soon as it was dark.

Aradus would have been amazed at how far he was from his uncle's thoughts. Lyconides's only concern at the moment was a sick young boy in the slave's quarters.

Aradus could hardly appreciate the soft bed he'd been given, such was his mental discomfort. He berated himself and his bad judgment for nearly an hour before he gave in to sleep. In repose his disfigured face softened so much he was nearly handsome again. With the worst side of his face turned into the scented pillow, an observer would never guess at his injuries. Yet such a small area of flesh had changed his life.

CHAPTER FIVE

The sun had risen high over the garrison walls before Aradus awoke. He found that thoughtful servants had laid out civilian clothes for him. He looked with dismay at the expensive toga, then carefully laid it aside. In a moment he was dressed in his uniform, his helmet under his arm.

Out in the hallway a woman was scrubbing the floor. She politely rose to her feet as Aradus approached.

"It's late. Has your master, Lyconides, left for the day?"

"Yes sir, he said you would understand. May I bring you some breakfast?" she asked.

"No, no need."

Aradus could never eat in the morning. Besides, he was too eager to be outdoors. He decided to give his horse a day's rest and walk about the town himself. Perhaps later in the day he could think of some plausible reason for cutting his visit short.

He took it personally that Lyconides had left without awakening him. Surely the older man wished to avoid him.

Aradus sighed as he put on his helmet.

"But then mine is hardly the face one wants at a breakfast table," he said to himself.

"Sir?" the woman inquired.

Aradus ignored her and made his way down the hall. Passing by the front room, he again noticed the large mirror on the wall. Stopping at a safe angle, he regarded it. The morning sunlight bounced off its surface and brightened the whole room. He was tempted only for a moment. Then with his face carefully turned, he walked out the door.

He didn't linger at the post but immediately left for town. He attracted a few stares as he strolled about, but mostly he had the streets to himself. The town was strangely quiet. He wondered at the lack of people. Yet another religious holiday, he decided.

After a while he tired of the hot streets and decided it would be more pleasant down by the seashore. As he neared the shore he was able to see why the town was so empty.

An immense crowd was gathered about the water. The soldier in him was alarmed. He feared these Jews were amassed for some revolt. But he quickly saw that there were more women and children there than men. No one seemed agitated or upset. The large crowd was very calm, listening intently to someone.

As he got closer, he was struck by how many fishing boats were docked and empty. What a perfect day this would be for fishing, he thought, yet no one was in the boats. Then he noticed one man standing in the bow of one of the docked boats. He was the speaker to whom the crowd was listening. When he was close enough, Aradus could hear the man's strong voice speaking above the gentle lapping of the waves. It was strangely soothing.

There were a few legionnaires scattered about the outer

fringes of the crowd. A good precaution, he thought. Aradus walked over to the closest soldier. The man instantly saluted, acknowledging the centurion. "Soldier, I'm stationed at Jerusalem," he said in a low voice, "What is all this?"

"Sir, that man is some sort of a religious teacher, a rabbi, I think," the man replied quietly. "These people will stand by the hour just to listen to Him."

"Really? It's about their religion? There's not some covert attempt at rebellion?"

"Not that we can tell, sir. Though we're watching it closely."

"To stand idle in the broiling sun! Leaving their work?" Aradus was amazed. He noticed the man shift uncomfortably.

"There's something else, soldier?"

A wave of disgust came over the man's plain face. "Well . . . they say He does things."

Never one to beg for information, Aradus calmly stared the man down.

"Sir, these clods claim He can heal people!" the soldier broke out loudly. "Not with medicine, mind you, but by waving His arms or something."

The man's sudden outburst attracted the irritated glances of several people. But after a black look from Aradus they quickly turned back to the man in the boat.

"His name wouldn't be Jesus?"

"You've heard of Him, then?"

Aradus didn't answer but looked back at the man in the boat. So this was Guni's friend. He had pictured some crafty charlatan dressed in outlandish clothes. This man looked so average.

Aradus was still too far away to make out all He was saying, but he could tell He was speaking in a calm, measured manner, only projecting His voice enough to raise over the lapping water. It was not at all like the dramatic theatrics employed by a conjurer.

Aradus dismissed the talk of healings as flagrant nonsense, rumors passed on by people too credulous and idle. He walked into the crowd to get a better look. He saw for the first time a small group of men arranged about the bow of the little boat. They leaned against it to help steady it. They would watch the man, then turn and gauge the crowd's reaction to what He said.

The man wants to lead something, Aradus thought. But what? Surely, He's not trying to gather an army out here in the open? Not with Roman soldiers looking on. Moving still closer, Aradus strained to catch what He was saying.

"Behold," Jesus said, "a sower went out to sow."

Farming, was the man talking about farming?

Aradus listened for a few minutes more but grew bored at what he perceived as a discourse on the best methods of planting. He walked back to the soldier.

"Well, sir, what did you think?" the man asked.

"These people don't have enough to do!" Shaking his head, he walked away puzzled.

As he walked back to the villa, he wondered if he really should cut his holiday short. This Jesus might bear watching.

He arrived at the barracks just as his uncle rode up on a fine black horse. When the older man stopped in front of him, Aradus took the beast's harness and examined its beautiful head.

"Hello, Aradus. Seeing the sights of Capernaum?" Lyconides asked as he dismounted.

"Yes. But I've seen nothing today to compare with this animal. See how his muzzle fits in my hand? He has to be an Arabian."

Lyconides was pleased at the praise of his favorite horse. "This is the finest one I've owned. I traded with a crafty old Bedouin in Damascus. Don't think he didn't try to cheat me."

"Did he?"

"Yes!" Lyconides laughed, giving the horse a gentle pat. "It was shameful, but you know how I love beautiful things."

"I'm sure he was worth the price . . . whatever it was. A good horse is worth ten soldiers. Men will fail you, but not a faithful mount."

Lyconides watched his nephew as he talked. He had changed so from the happy, gregarious boy he used to be. He was bitter. In all his talking last night he had never mentioned any friends or asked after the family. He had politely refused to talk of his injuries.

It struck Lyconides as odd that of all the packets of mail he received from relatives in Rome none had ever mentioned Aradus's face. Now that he thought of it, the letters had barely mentioned his nephew for the last two years. What had happened?

After stabling the horse, the two men returned to Lyconides's household. Drusus appeared at the doorway. His face was anxious. Lyconides approached him quickly.

"What is it, Drusus?"

"Master, Avva is so ill. Nothing we've done seems to help. His mother is beside herself with worry."

"Let me see." Lyconides walked to the slave's quarters with Aradus following. They entered a small chamber where an older woman was hovering about a bed. On the bed lay Avva. How different the boy looked today. His blond hair lay in damp clumps upon his forehead; his blue eyes seemed sunken and unfocused.

The woman was very relieved to see Lyconides. "Master.

Thank you for coming. Avva grows worse by the hour."

"What's wrong with him?"

"I don't know, Master. It seems to be some sort of fever." She paused to lay a loving hand on the boy's brow. "But nothing I've done has been any help."

Lyconides looked gravely at the boy. He thought for a moment, then turned to the doorway. "Drusus."

"Yes, sir."

"Run down to camp and ask the physician to come."

Drusus looked surprised but left without hesitation. Aradus was a little surprised himself. He wondered if the camp physician would trouble himself over a slave.

"Daphne, we are only crowding you here. I'll send the physician in as soon as he arrives," Lyconides said.

The woman gave him her heartfelt thanks, then turned to resume her anxious watch over her son.

The two men left her to have a light meal while waiting for the physician. Aradus ate well, but Lyconides barely picked at his food; his ears strained for the sound of the approaching physician.

They had finished the meal before Drusus returned with the man. He apparently did not share any sense of urgency. He was older than Lyconides, though his closely cut hair was still blue black.

Lyconides rose to meet him. "Tibullus, you are doing me a great favor by coming here."

"Yes, I know," he said languidly. Tibullus waited for an invitation to sit down, but it was not forthcoming. Lyconides gently took him by the elbow to steer him in the right direction.

"The boy is gravely ill, so I'll show you to him. Aradus will excuse us, I know." Without waiting for a reply, Lyconides guided the man out of the room, ignoring the surprised and disgruntled look on his face.

"Well done, Uncle," Aradus said softly as he raised a goblet in a toast. For lack of anything else to do, Aradus decided to wait and hear the prognosis.

His wait was a very short one. In scarcely more than a quarter hour, he heard the sounds of voices in the hallway.

Tibullus was talking as they entered the room. "I tell you, I've seen this too many times."

"You're sure? There couldn't be a mistake?"

Tibullus was silent, a picture of affronted pride.

"Oh, forgive me," Lyconides said tiredly as he placed a hand on the man's shoulder. "I'm being very rude. I know you're right. I just don't want to believe it. Please. Sit with us a while."

Mollified, the physician smiled and sat down on the nearest couch. "I can understand your frustration. Decent slaves are hard to come by. He would have grown up to have been a handsome indoor servant. I've never seen a blond Jew before."

"His mother's a Celt. After I bought her she became a Jew and married Drusus, Avva's father."

"Well, perhaps they'll have more, and you can recoup your loss."

Lyconides was silent, looking intently at the floor. Aradus looked at the drawn face of his uncle, then turned to Tibullus. "What's wrong with him?"

"Brain fever. Not a thing I can do. It's already turning into palsy."

"Palsy?"

"Yes, you can expect him to have a partial or total loss of sensibility and voluntary motion. In this case I'm expecting the worst. I've never seen it come on so fast." He spoke the dire news calmly, wondering when Lyconides was going to offer him some wine.

"Of course, that's not the worst part."

Lyconides jerked his head up.

"There's more?"

"Afraid so. Sorry, but the slave won't die. Not only have you lost the worth of him, you'll be stuck caring for the twitching whelp."

Aradus saw a large vein come out on his uncle's neck as the man clamped his jaw shut in anger. Tibullus, however, was quite oblivious to the emotions he was engaging. He laid his well-cared-for hands on the table and continued talking in a lower tone. "However, a lot can happen to an ill slave. Why throw good money after bad, eh? Especially if just a small sum could buy you a different kind of medicine."

Lyconides was too angry to speak. Curious, Aradus asked, "What kind of medicine?"

"Well . . . let's just say that while it wouldn't cure the slave it would certainly cure the problem. Permanently."

Silence hung in the air like a heavy weight. When Tibullas finally saw that Lyconides was not going to speak, he shrugged his shoulders. He rose from the table and began to straighten his expensive woolen cloak.

He calmly looked into Lyconides's burning black eyes. "Some men can be stationed too long in a province. They get too used to the people. They become familiar with those they came to conquer. They even get attached to them. It's not good for the empire. It's not good for the Roman who so forgets himself."

After that little speech, Tibullus nodded to Aradus and walked out. Aradus was silent, watching him go.

"The toad! Death is the only cure he can offer?" Lyconides spoke in a low, harsh voice, barely reaching his nephew's ears.

CHAPTER SIX

*T*he next day Aradus awoke in time to have breakfast with his uncle. The older man was preoccupied. Still, he struggled to be polite for his nephew's sake. "So, my boy, what are your plans for the day?"

"I thought to catch up on some much neglected reading. I don't wish to stoop to the level of the barbarians, even if I am in this illiterate province."

"Why do you say illiterate?"

"Well, Uncle, you'd hardly find a Cicero or a Virgil among these Jews."

"Perhaps, but don't forget these are the 'People of the Law.' Their whole life is based on the writings of their forefathers. You really must read their Psalms, as fine a work as any of Homer's poems."

"I can't read Hebrew."

"No matter, I have a Greek translation."

As Aradus finished his meal, he thought of what Tibullus had said last night. Was his uncle becoming too close to the Jews? Too attached to the people and their ways?

His worry increased as he walked into the room his uncle had set aside for a library. Nearly half the scrolls were in Hebrew; those that weren't appeared to be concerned with some aspect of Jewish life or law. As Lyconides bustled about his favorite room, showing off treasured works, Aradus studied him. He seemed more scholar than soldier. Both men had come from a cultured, aristocratic family. Their training for the military had not precluded an extensive education. Still, such a wealth of materials went far beyond intellectual curiosity. This was bordering on an obsession.

"I must leave for camp, Aradus, but this should keep you busy for a while."

"Indeed. Thank you, you're a thoughtful host."

Aradus took the scroll of Psalms his uncle offered and sat down. His uncle went to the door, then paused. He turned again to the younger man. "Aradus, if anything . . . if anything should change with Avva, will you send for me?"

"Of course, Uncle."

Lyconides's dark eyes looked intently at his nephew. He wondered if he could make the young man understand him. "I always dreamed of having children, Aradus. Especially sons. Perhaps I see something in Avva. Something I might have had if my world had been a different one."

It struck Aradus how little he knew his uncle. He had no reply for him.

Looking very sad, Lyconides left for his day's work.

Aradus opened the scroll and began to read. He noted the line, "But his delight is in the law of the LORD, and in His law he meditates day and night."

"Their precious law! It pervades their every thought," he murmured to himself.

"'I will not be afraid of ten thousands of people, that have set themselves against me round about.' Hah! That doesn't sound like any Jews I've met."

He continued to read, making occasional comments for some time. His uncle was right, though; this was quite good. The form surprised him. Truly it could stand up to the classics he had been schooled in. He disagreed violently with the content, though.

"'For I will not trust in my bow, neither shall my sword save me.' What a thought. As if there were anything else to trust in this life."

He read through the morning, often shaking his head in disagreement, but was not able to put the scroll down. When he finished the Psalms he picked up other translated Jewish scrolls. They angered and fascinated him.

Great was his surprise when after many hours of study, his uncle appeared in the doorway. "Uncle, home so soon?"

"So soon? The morning is spent and the afternoon is nearly done. Ah, these illiterate Jews have held you here all this time."

Aradus gave him a rueful grin and stood up to stretch. Shaking his head, he held out the scroll he held in his hand.

"I disagree with everything they say. But I will concede they make a wondrously good argument."

A smile of great satisfaction spread across Lyconides's face. "What do you disagree with?"

"Where do I start? Only one God? Angels? Miracles? Life after death?"

"You don't believe in life after death?"

"'When soul and body out of which we're formed, One entity, Are torn apart in death, Nothing can touch our sense at all, Or move our consciousness.'"

"Bah! Don't go quoting Lucretius to me. I could never stand him or his philosophy."

"Why is that?" Aradus asked, chagrined at such censure of his favorite writer.

"The man would mouth such lofty thoughts while he was locked away in a scholar's world. He totally ignored the great civil wars being fought all around him. A writer must speak, not just to men, but to their condition. He must address a man's life."

Lyconides gently took the scroll from his nephew's hand. He held it up between them. "Aradus, this speaks to me. This is about real life, real men and women."

"Jewish men and women."

The sound of running feet kept Lyconides from replying. He turned to see Daphne hurrying towards him. His face blanched as he saw her. "Daphne what's wrong?"

"Master! Avva's fallen from the bed."

The two men quickly returned with her to the boy's room. The sight that met them touched even Aradus's hard heart. The boy lay sprawled in a heap on the floor, the right half of his body shaking violently.

"Avva," Lyconides murmured sorrowfully as he knelt beside him.

The boy tried unsuccessfully to lift his head, but his muscles would not obey. "I . . . m-m-must . . . w-w-work," he stammered with great effort.

Amazed, Aradus saw moisture gathering in his uncle's eyes. Tears for a slave?

With little effort, the two men lifted the boy and returned him to his bed.

Lyconides looked at the ruined form on the bed. As a soldier he had seen many young men die, an awful necessity he had reconciled himself to. But this, to be worse than crippled, this was a travesty. Making a decision, Lyconides turned to Daphne. "Do you know where He is today?"

Daphne looked uncertain for a moment, then answered. "I heard He was up on the mount."

Without hesitation, Lyconides left the room. Shooting a look of puzzlement at the woman, Aradus followed his uncle. "Sir, where are you going?"

"To the mount, to find Him," he answered shortly, not breaking his stride.

"But surely, a servant can fetch Drusus for you."

"I am not looking for Drusus."

"Who, then?"

Lyconides stopped at the front door. He studied his nephew, wondering if he could make him understand. "Aradus, we have not seen each other for many years. You're greatly changed from the boy I knew. I've changed in ways you may not understand . . . or like."

Aradus waited.

"That . . . slave was born here in this house. I've watched him grow up. I care greatly for the child. And he cares greatly for me. Yes, even though he knows I could trade him in a moment for a good horse or so many barrels of oil. Don't I owe him something? Something besides buying a 'medicine' to help him die?"

Lyconides waited for an answer, but Aradus had none to give. Placing his hands on his lean hips, Lyconides looked at the floor for a moment, then back at Aradus. "You don't have an answer for me. Neither did our great skilled physician. I'm going to someone who just might be able to do something. I'm going to Jesus."

"You can't!"

"You were the one who told me the stories of His healing people."

"But that's all they were! Stories! Stories told by children to amuse each other. Why, even some of the children didn't believe in Him."

"I don't care. I have to try something!" With that, he went outside, Aradus still following.

"Wait. Think of your position, Uncle!"

Lyconides gave him an impatient look over his shoulder but continued walking. Exasperated, Aradus fell into step beside him. Their long strides took them quickly to the edge of town, where they saw a great deal of people gathered.

"He must have returned from the mount," Lyconides commented.

Aradus bit back his reply as he came to an abrupt stop. "Uncle, look there!" he exclaimed, pointing to a filthy old man just a few paces away. "Uncle, it's a leper! What can he mean by coming into town!"

"And look at the fools pressing against him!" Lyconides then called out to the man, "You there! Stop! What do you mean by this outrage?"

The people turned to face the Romans, then backed away in fear. The man was suddenly alone in the middle of a large circle of people. He turned his tear streaked face towards Lyconides, then took a few tentative steps towards him.

Aradus had his sword out in a moment. "Back! Back, you piece of filth, or I'll drop you where you stand."

Terrified, the man moved back. Lyconides put his hand on Aradus's arm to calm him. He spoke to the man in a firm voice. "Do you wish to infect these people with your rotting flesh? Would you have them to suffer leprosy too?"

The man looked at Lyconides again as he began to shake with violent sobbing. He slowly lifted his hands toward the sky as he continued to be racked with his weeping. "I have no leprosy!" he shouted. "I have been healed!"

The two centurions noticed then the skin that showed between the beggar's rags. It was pink and firm. There wasn't a blotch or blemish to be seen.

"What?" Aradus growled. "Make sense, man."

"He healed me. He healed me!"

"Where is He?" Lyconides demanded.

Several people looked suspiciously at the Romans, but the man was oblivious to anything except his joy. He pointed to a small group of men walking away toward the hills.

Without another word, Aradus and Lyconides walked toward the group, the crowd parting as the two Roman soldiers came through.

"Please," Lyconides called out. "Please wait."

Aradus ground his teeth in frustration at his uncle's politeness. But it had the desired effect. The group stopped and waited for the two men to catch up.

All the men in the group looked nervous except for one. Lyconides walked toward Him. He was as tall as Lyconides but heavier. He looked to be someone who had worked all His life and worked hard.

Like the group of men with Him, His brown hair was short and His beard was neat. The only thing that made Him stand out was His calmness.

Lyconides saw compassion in the man's large brown eyes. It caused him to lose any doubts he might have had. "Lord, my servant lies at home paralyzed, dreadfully tormented."

Aradus winced at his uncle calling this Jew "Lord," but he held his tongue. He was fascinated by what was unfolding.

Jesus simply nodded, a kind smile on His face. "I will come and heal him."

"Lord, I am not worthy that You should come under my roof. But speak a word only, and my servant will be healed. For I am a man under authority; I have soldiers under me who do whatever I say."

Jesus nearly laughed with delight. He gave Lyconides a hearty pat on the back, then turned to face the crowd. "Truly, I tell you, I have not found such great faith! No, not even in Israel."

Jesus sobered then and talked to the assembled people in a different, sadder tone. "Many will come from the east and west, and will sit down with Abraham, Isaac, and Jacob, in the kingdom of heaven. But the children of the kingdom will be cast out into outer darkness. There will be weeping and gnashing of teeth."

Placing His hand on the Roman's arm, Jesus told him gently, "Go your way, and as you have believed, so let it be done for you."

As the two Romans walked back through the crowds they were a study in contrasts. Lyconides's elegant face was lit by a glowing smile. Aradus's damaged visage was further marred by a scowling frown.

Aradus was eaten up with anger and shame. His uncle had played the fool before the whole town. He had not just treated the Jew as an equal but had called Him "Lord"!

It was more than disgusting; it was dangerous. His uncle would be in serious trouble if his superiors found out. Perhaps Aradus would be questioned for associating with him.

No word passed between the two men as they returned to the barracks. Each was busy with his own thoughts—Lyconides with happy expectations, Aradus vowing to leave at the first light of dawn.

As they drew near his uncle's quarters, they saw the doors were all open, with soldiers and servants clustered about. Lyconides began to run at the sight, pushing his way through into the rooms. Aradus followed at a dignified pace, then stopped at the sight in the hallway. Lyconides was embracing a strong, healthy Avva.

Everyone in the household was talking and laughing, including Avva, who now spoke without the trace of a stutter. Aradus watched from the doorway as all tried to tell at once what they had seen. When Lyconides began to relate his own experience, Aradus walked away.

As he entered the library, he realized his anger had been replaced by confusion, the greatest confusion he had ever known. Picking up one of the Jewish scrolls, he began to read.

CHAPTER SEVEN

*J*ust as Aradus had promised himself, he left his uncle's place before dawn. It had been very easy to slip away in all the happy confusion of the household.

It was unspeakable for him to leave that way. He felt his rudeness keenly. Still, there was something about the whole business with the boy that drove him away. He couldn't have borne another day in the place.

His whole world had tilted. He couldn't understand what had happened to the boy. He couldn't understand his uncle's strange behavior. He only knew that he wanted to put as many miles between himself and Capernaum as possible.

He rode the long journey straight through, resting his horse only when necessary. He rode around Nazareth, not wanting to meet the little Jewish boy again. He rode until he saw the walls of Jerusalem.

There was no relief in the sight, though. He felt a great weight descend on his spirit as the city came into view.

He passed by the hill of Golgotha on his way into the city.

He could tell at a glance that there would be crucifixions that day.

Golgotha was a small lump of a hill just a short distance from the city. Cypress trees lined its base, but the side facing the city was bare. This forced anyone coming or going from Jerusalem that way to witness the harshness of Roman rule.

It had always been the Roman custom to leave crucified bodies to rot on their crosses as foul carrion for vultures and buzzards. But this did not happen in Judea. As a rare concession to Jewish law, the dead criminals were removed and disposed of by their people. Hence, Golgotha was a relatively clean place compared to most crucifixion sites.

He rode silently past the group of soldiers and their prisoners as they made their way up the hill. He nodded at a fellow centurion, glad he did not have the gruesome duty that day.

He entered the western gate of the city by Herod the Great's palace. The Romans had taken over this structure for their own use. The governor Pilate would stay there whenever he came to Jerusalem. It was a beautiful set of buildings, surpassed only by the high priest's palace and, of course, the Temple.

The complex was more than 750 feet in length. At the northern end of the compound were barracks for the troops. The palace itself was made of two large villas facing each other. Each villa was capable of holding hundreds of people. A large courtyard separated the two villas, and the courtyard contained large areas of landscaping with bronze reflecting ponds.

As Aradus rode towards the barracks he heard a voice calling his name from the courtyard. Turning, Aradus saw it was the legate Marcus Livius, his direct superior. Aradus stopped his horse and dismounted. Walking up to the man, he gave him a stiff salute. Aradus took care to hide the loathing he felt for this man.

The legate returned the salute, then smiled broadly. He was glad of Aradus's return. Some nasty business had occurred while the centurion was gone, business that could have caused no end of trouble. As he saw the young man, a plan began to form in the legate's mind. Yes, Aradus would do nicely.

Marcus Livius knew how to grasp opportunities. He had a reputation for coming through unscathed in the worst situations. He also had a reputation for letting others pay for his survival.

Every aspect of his life had been kissed with success. Family, stature, wealth—Livius had them all. Physically, he was a tall, handsome man. He possessed unusual golden eyes that fascinated any woman he cared to look at. His black hair framed a nearly perfect face. He used his attributes in any way that he could. He had discovered that people would trust a smiling, handsome man whether they had any reason to or not. He had used this fact well.

He had an ironic sense of humor that thinly covered his basic dearth of character. He was seldom in a bad mood, presenting a jovial countenance to the world. Only subordinates like Aradus knew that Livius was at his most dangerous when he was smiling. So it was with great foreboding that Aradus saw how eager the legate was to see him.

"Centurion, back so soon? I thought you planned to stay longer."

"There was illness in the household," Aradus said simply.

"Really? I'm sorry to hear it. Though you couldn't have returned at a better time. You are just the man I wanted to see."

Aradus felt a sinking feeling as he watched the handsome face. Livius didn't explain further, but lightly touching the centurion's arm he led him from the courtyard and toward the barracks.

"Go settle in at the barracks, Aradus. Then come to my quarters sometime this evening. We can talk so much better there." He had spoken with an elaborate casualness. Then with an affable nod, he strode away, humming a popular camp song.

Aradus cursed.

The centurion's return to the barracks was greeted with surly looks from the men assigned to him. They had greatly enjoyed his absence.

There wasn't an actual Roman legion stationed in Jerusalem, but a contingent of auxiliaries. Auxiliaries were soldiers from the conquered provinces—Gauls, Britons, and other colonials who had either volunteered or been pressed into service for the empire. The auxiliaries were yet another concession to the Jews, who could not abide too many pig-eating Romans in their holy city.

These auxiliaries were commanded by centurions such as Aradus. He was a Roman from the soles of his sandals to the hook in his nose.

He waited until the sun had set for the evening, then made his way to Livius's quarters. The legate had a building set off for himself at a distance from the barracks that had been decorated with elaborate ostentation. Not a few of his furnishings were said to be grateful gifts from the Temple priests, with whom he had a good working relationship.

Livius called out for Aradus to enter, just as soon as he had knocked. He had obviously been waiting for him, despite the earliness of the hour.

Aradus entered and stood for a moment as his eyes

adjusted to the bright light of the interior. There were two bronze braziers in the corners and several large, expensive candles about. It was unusual to have so much light at night. The legate even had an oil lamp burning on the table.

The centurion blinked, then saw that Livius was watching him from the low couch by the table. Livius was reclining on his left elbow, his right hand holding a large silver goblet. He was dressed in a long white toga trimmed in a thin band of purple.

Livius cocked his head to one side, studying Aradus. "Still in uniform, centurion?"

"I thought you had duties for me."

"Of course. Though I do give you permission to remove your helmet."

Aradus complied and stood there in the bright light bareheaded. He knew he was being toyed with, but to what purpose?

Livius smiled, fixing his golden eyes on the man's injuries. "There, isn't that so much better?"

"Yes, sir," Aradus said stiffly.

"Certain developments have occurred while you were in Capernaum. Governor Pilate has made plans to decorate the ramparts of Herod's palace."

As he talked, Livius didn't look Aradus in the eye but stared at the deformed part of his face. It was a deliberate action that, along with the bright light, made it hard for the younger man to attend properly to what the legate was saying.

"Pilate has ordered gilded shields from Rome to be sent here to adorn the palace. Of course, they will have only certain inscriptions on them, no images that would break the Jews' precious commandments.

"Still, you know how touchy these people can be, so we're to be very low key about the whole business. When the shields arrive in four months, just put them up without any fanfare."

Livius talked in a very bored fashion as if the news were hardly worth telling. Yet his gaze never wavered from the man's injuries.

Always self-conscious about his ruined face, Aradus had become angry. He wished for the interview to be over.

Livius stopped talking, as if what he was looking at was too distracting. Aradus was forced to endure his rudeness until he made a great show of recollecting himself.

"Oh. What was I saying? I guess that was about it. I wonder if you could do me a small favor, though," Livius said pleasantly, his eyes finally shifting to meet the centurion's stony gaze.

"Yes, sir."

"I had some small business with the chief priests that I need to reply to. I really hate to make you a messenger boy, but there you are, still in uniform." Livius laughed. "I really can't help but take advantage of you."

Aradus was too angry to let the words sink in, and the legate knew it. He sat up on the couch and set his goblet down on the table. Taking a plain waxed tablet from the table, Livius held it out to the centurion. "If you would be good enough to run this up to Caiaphas, the high priest, I would be so grateful."

"Yes, sir."

Another time Aradus would have wondered why a vain man like Livius would use such a plain tablet for a message to the high priest. He would also have wondered why the wax wafer holding the tablet shut didn't contain the man's seal. But as he saluted and left, he could only think of the sound of the man's laughter when he had shut the door.

CHAPTER EIGHT

The palace of the high priest had been another great testimony to Herod the Great's building frenzy. It was hard by the western wall of the city about three hundred yards from the southern gate.

As Aradus approached the outer courtyard, a knot of Jewish palace guards quickly stepped forward to meet him. The centurion looked at them in disdain, then glanced over their heads to see other guards stationed at the doors to the palace and around the porticos leading to the two side yards. He grimaced at this brave showing of guards. He felt that five of his highly trained men could subdue the whole lot.

He calmly announced his business.

One of the older guards tried to stare Aradus down. When he saw it would never work, he blustered at a young man beside him, "Well, go on, then!"

The young man left the group to enter the palace. The others stayed clustered near Aradus as if he might be considering a one-man assault on the place. He looked at them in derision.

Presently, a small cluster of richly robed men appeared in the palace doorway. They filed slowly out into the courtyard, eyeing the Roman suspiciously. An elderly man leaning on a gold-banded staff motioned to Aradus.

Aradus dismounted and threw the reins to one of the guards. As he approached the group, he could see that two men were even better dressed than the others, the elderly man and another man in his fifties.

The centurion inclined his head in a short nod. "You are the high priest?" he asked the old man.

The man was hard to look at despite his sumptuous clothes. The brightly lit torches of the courtyard made his sallow skin look as yellow as butter. His flesh clung in loose folds on his jowls and neck. Eyes that were rheumy and jaundiced stared from twin caverns set in his face. Thin wisps of yellow-white beard still clung to his ancient chin. Despite his heavy perfumes, the stench from his rotting teeth was nearly unbearable. "I am Annas!" he announced.

The middle-aged man came forward. His appearance was a stark contrast to the ancient beside him. This man was well fed. His face was smooth and ruddy. Iron gray hair, full and curly, covered his head. His still black beard neatly framed his jaw. "I am Caiaphas, the high priest. What is your business with me?"

"A message," Aradus said as he handed over the tablet. He wondered as he saw the high priest's face light up. It struck him suddenly that the high priest and his entourage had all come out to meet him.

Caiaphas took the tablet and moved a few paces from the others toward a blazing torch set in the ground. His father-in-law, Annas, moved with him.

The two read in silence for a moment, then looked at each other. Without a word, Caiaphas opened the tablet wide so that it faced the intense heat of the torch. In a moment, the wax smoothed out, obliterating the message.

Annas beckoned to the other men with his gnarled hand. With surprising animation for his age, he walked back to the palace, the men trailing in his wake.

Caiaphas stayed by the torch, stroking his soft beard and watching the centurion. "Any reply?" Aradus asked.

The high priest looked surprised at the question. Then a small, knowing smile came to his face. "No . . . no, I hardly think so." He handed the tablet back to Aradus, then left to join the others in the palace.

As Aradus walked back to his horse, he noted how chilly the night was becoming. Jerusalem is 2,500 feet above the sea, so even the most beautiful spring days could turn uncomfortably cold.

After seating his horse, he wrapped his scarlet wool cloak about his shoulders, comforted by the fact that these surly guards would be spending the night in the open courtyard.

It was the only comfort he had. As he rode through the dark streets, alone with his thoughts, he began to consider what the legate had told him. He wished now he had been more alert and not so concerned with the man's rude staring.

How could Livius think the Jews wouldn't be upset by Roman shields on the palace ramparts? There had been rioting when Pilate had brought imperial standards into Jerusalem.

The Jews lived in subjection, it was true. But they had made it very clear from the first that there were some things they would die for. Keeping their holy city pure from pagan symbols was one of them. The empire had learned in dealing with the Jews when to push and when to give. Making exceptions for their religious zeal had worked very well over the years.

The empire and the Jewish leaders had an uneasy partnership that Governor Pilate had threatened almost since the moment he had taken office. First, by bringing the Roman standards into the city, then by raiding the Temple treasury. Both incidents had led to violence and upheavals. Aradus had not been stationed in Jerusalem at the time, but he had heard enough about the situations to wonder at Pilate's administration. It had always been Roman policy to keep things as smooth as possible, yet Pilate often went out of his way to provoke these people.

Which again led his thoughts to Livius. How could so cunning a man be so cavalier about Pilate's latest decision? These gilded shields would be another slap in the face to the Jews. Didn't he say they would be inscribed? With what? He knew anything the Romans would write on the shields would be interpreted as more pagan influence.

Aradus stopped his horse in the middle of the street. No, anything he could think of, Livius would be two steps ahead of him. Aradus furrowed his brow in concentration, then turned to look back at the high priest's palace. What had he done?

He had been the go-between for the double-dealing Livius. Of course the legate had been concerned. More rioting and violence would have hurt his dealings with the Temple vanguard, the Jewish elite who kept him comfortable. He had been so concerned, he had tipped them off this very night.

Aradus cursed Livius, then himself. If only he hadn't been so preoccupied with his looks, he could have seen the web Livius had spun for him. With his own hands he had informed the Jews of Pilate's newest edict, giving them the chance to thwart it in some way. Not that that wouldn't be a good thing. Still, what would Pilate do to Aradus if he ever found out?

When Aradus returned to the legate's quarters he had to pound for some time before Livius deigned to open the door. At last, he did so, releasing the pungent smells of wine and burning tallow into the night air.

Livius's normally clear eyes were bleary and vague looking. He had trouble focusing on the centurion's face. After a moment of confused squinting, a broad smile broke across his face. "Ah, centurion," he said thickly. "Still up and about serving our glorious empire?"

"I delivered your message."

Laughing in his face, Livius splayed his hands across his chest. He looked about in playful surprise. "My message? Surely you have mistaken me for some other . . . well, I guess there aren't any other legates here, are there? Still, there is some mistake. I would hardly use such a dignified centurion as yourself for an errand boy."

"You know—"

Livius interrupted him with another loud burst of laughter. Shaking his head, he shut the door in Aradus's face, smiling all the while.

CHAPTER NINE

As the days turned into weeks, a growing discontentment began to fill Aradus's life. Long distrustful of people, he had placed all his loyalties and energies in his service to the empire.

He had taken a great deal of satisfaction in his duties, his position. Being a centurion didn't flatter his vanity; it had completed him. Never a conceited man, he had seen the dignity of his position as a tool, something that would further his efficiency.

That was changing. The legate now made a great show of ignoring him. This open disfavor made the other centurions avoid him, and it made his own men restless.

Aradus only worked that much harder. As the months passed, he drilled his men, pushing them as hard as he was pushing himself. He knew when the shields finally did arrive from Rome, he and his men would be called upon to quell the ensuing revolt.

He made it his business to be at headquarters when any dispatches arrived from Rome. Strangely, though, no mention was ever made of the shields.

Four months came and went without their arrival. Aradus kept working his men, certain it was just a matter of time.

Late one hot summer night, as Aradus lay stretched out on his hard bed, too uncomfortable to sleep, he could hear the sound of heavy sandals along the hallway. Someone was approaching.

Aradus sat up and put a foot on the floor. The shields have finally arrived, he reasoned.

He rose from his bed when the footsteps stopped outside of his quarters.

The centurion opened the door before anyone could knock. He found himself face to face with Marcus Livius. The legate looked nearly as surprised as Aradus.

"Ever the vigilant soldier, I see," Livius commented dryly, as he slid past the door and into the room.

Livius held a small oil lamp that barely illuminated three feet in front of him. He motioned for Aradus to shut the door, then held the lamp up to inspect the sparse room. He shook his head, then held the light towards Aradus.

He examined the centurion with a close scrutiny, knowing it was the best way to nettle the man. Aradus wore only a simple linen toga in deference to the heat. He had also shaved his hair close for the summer, accentuating his misshapen face. Despite his bulging muscles, Aradus looked vulnerable without his armor and helmet.

"Why, Aradus, you are a turtle out of his shell. I had supposed you slept in full dress uniform, propped in a corner, awaiting the dawn."

Aradus didn't bother to answer such banter, knowing Livius would come to the point of his visit in his own good time.

Taking the only chair in the room, the legate sat down, placing the lamp on the floor beside him. He waved toward the bed in the corner. "Do sit down, Aradus. I promise not to tell anyone that you are actually lax enough to own a bed."

"Yes, sir."

After Aradus was seated, Livius leaned back in the chair. He planted his large feet far apart and placed his hands on his knees. He gave every indication of someone planning on a long visit.

The lighting was poor, but Aradus could still dimly make out the legate. He sat and smiled at Aradus in a most friendly way—not saying anything, just smiling.

He was indulging his odd sense of humor, Aradus knew. This was his way of toying with the centurion, feeling the power that he had over him. Finally, the legate sighed deeply. "Pity that the light is so weak in this little hole. I so enjoy talking face to face. Of course, you might not mind the darkness as much as I, eh, centurion?"

Aradus was silent.

"Well, in any case, I thought you would want to know that the shields have arrived."

Blinking in surprise, Aradus watched the legate. He had been expecting this news, but Livius's calm, cheerful demeanor threw him. What did this man know?

Leaning back even further, Livius looked at the ceiling. He was a picture of satisfaction. "They have arrived . . . but not in Jerusalem. An imperial edict has sent them to Caesarea where they will be dedicated to the Temple of Augustus."

"How did this happen?"

Livius snapped his head back down and gave his most charming grin. "It seems a concerned officer, a centurion we think, tipped off the high priest. The Jews, in turn, sent a petition signed by the Herodian prince to Caesar himself."

Aradus's eyes grew wide.

"Caesar's response has been as swift as it was angry. He accused Pilate of crassly violating established policies concerning local customs."

Sitting very still, Aradus waited for the rest.

"As you can imagine Pilate is furious. But rather than admit he was wrong, he's blaming everything on this centurion . . . whoever he is."

Aradus's mouth became quite dry.

"It seems a Roman soldier was spotted leaving the high priest's palace one night last spring. No one would have known his rank in the darkness, but the poor fool made a show of his red centurion cloak. Believe me, I don't envy the man if Pilate finds him."

Aradus stood up, consumed with rage. His mind was roiling with one thought, to knock the grinning legate to the floor. The centurion was an evil sight as the small flame of the lamp made fearful shadows on his deformed face.

Livius only laughed.

"You are becoming quite emotional, centurion. Perhaps it is this dreadful heat. It occurs to me you could stand a change."

He fearlessly looked up into the man's burning eyes. With a greatly exaggerated show of surprise, he exclaimed, "I know, Aradus! You could oversee the shields' dedication in Caesarea. Think of it. Caesarea, a real Roman city. Fresh sea breezes cooling the summer air. Public baths, real food . . . ah, I really am too good to my men." The legate's brilliant eyes danced in the lamplight. He was enjoying himself immensely.

"Caesarea is also the official residence of Pilate," Aradus ground out.

"Why, so it is," Livius agreed. "Does that concern you in some way?"

Beside himself with impotent fury, Aradus could only clench his fists. He knew there was still a slim chance of surviving Livius's machinations, if only he could keep his mouth shut. It was costing him dearly, though.

Livius waited a few heartbeats, then smiled even more broadly. He had achieved all his ends. Despite his goading, the centurion would keep silent in order to salvage his career.

Aradus could only stand there, beaten.

Still smiling, Livius slowly got up from the chair. He stretched, then patted the centurion on the back. "I knew how delighted you would be at the prospect, so I've made arrangements for you to leave tonight. Now, in fact. There's a fresh horse and rations waiting for you at the Eastern Gate. When you get to Caesarea, go to the Temple of Augustus and ask for the centurion Cornelius. He'll help you with all the details. I know how eager you are to do this right, so take your time."

Livius paused to furrow his brows as if in deep thought. "I'd say this should keep you occupied at least until Passover. Yes, don't come back until Passover week. By then . . . well, let's just say Pilate should have forgotten about that loose-lipped centurion."

"That's also the week Pilate will return to Jerusalem for the Jews' holidays," Aradus said with a stone face.

"Hmm? Why so it is," Livius laughed. "But again, what is that to you?" Laughing again, Livius walked to the door. "You needn't thank me, centurion. Serving the empire is my only reward."

After the legate left, Aradus quickly dressed and packed his meager belongings in his pack. As he picked up his dagger he could feel the medallion of honor that had been placed there so many years ago. Yes, an honored warrior of the state, and here he was being forced to slink away in the night like a common thief.

CHAPTER TEN

Caesarea was nearly seventy miles from Jerusalem, on the coast of the Mediterranean sea. The four-day journey was not one a person would wish to take in the heat of the summer, especially with metal and leather for clothing.

Hardship was no stranger to Aradus, however. Despite his great discomfort, he made his way to the city as quickly as possible. He wondered all the while what would meet him there. Had Livius spun another web of duplicity? Would Pilate have guards waiting for him at the gates?

It was a game to Livius to put him in such close proximity to the angry Pilate. The legate enjoyed making others nervous. Still, if Pilate was looking for a centurion in Jerusalem he really might be safer here. Plus, what could Livius gain by Aradus being discovered? There was always the chance Aradus would tell who wrote the message, and the chance that Pilate would believe him.

The more Aradus thought about it, the more convinced he became that Livius was truly trying to keep Pilate from noticing him. It made him feel less apprehensive, but not a whit less angry.

With welcome relief, Aradus finally saw the city shimmering in the distant heat. He rode toward it feeling that whatever waited for him there could not be much worse than the broiling desert.

Caesarea was a jewel of civilization set out in the middle of a wasteland. It had received all the benefits of a man's vanities, that man being Herod the Great. He had lavished twelve years of his attentions upon it.

His mania for building had known no bounds. In Caesarea, his energies had provided the city with a tower, a temple, a theater, and an amphitheater. There was a complete system of aqueducts and drainage. He had even built an artificial harbor that was as fine as the great harbor at Athens.

Herod had named the place after his patron, Augustus Caesar, and it had soon become the Roman capital of Palestine. It was also, as Aradus could not forget, the official residence of Governor Pilate.

Aradus entered the city's southern gate, trying hard to look calm, and as inconspicuous as his horse and size would allow. He rode straight ahead, almost as if he knew where he was going. He didn't. But he would not show his confusion for the world.

Surely, he reasoned, even in a city like this, a temple dedicated to Augustus would be hard to miss. Livius had neglected to give him any directions, probably by design. And Aradus did not want to draw undue attention to himself by appearing to be a stranger in need of help.

As he rode down street after street, he vowed that if there was an afterlife, he would spend it hunting down Marcus Livius.

"Centurion!"

A voice called out from the corner, interrupting his black thoughts. Aradus reined in his horse and turned to look at another centurion who was approaching.

The man was older and much shorter than Aradus. He walked with a calm dignity that more than made up for his small stature. He approached Aradus and offered a salute. "Hail Caesar."

"Hail Caesar."

"May I gather that you have just come from Jerusalem?"

Instantly on the alert, Aradus eyed the man warily, wondering what his intent was. "Why do you ask?"

The other man raised his gray eyebrows high over his amber eyes. Aradus's rough tone had surprised him. "I am Cornelius. I was to meet a centurion from Jerusalem today," he said mildly. He had a very deep voice that carried well over the din of the street.

Aradus nearly smiled, he was so relieved. Without answering he dismounted. Stiff from his time in the saddle, he stretched his sore back. He looked down at Cornelius, wondering how much he knew about Pilate and the shields. "I am from Jerusalem," he admitted finally.

Cornelius had too much patience to be annoyed at the younger man. He also had far too much self-confidence to be intimidated by Aradus's glowering presence. He did wonder, though, what emotion was consuming the man. "Do you wish to go to the temple now?"

Aradus wished to go to bed, but he answered, "Yes."

Cornelius pointed down a side street, and the two men began to walk. Despite himself, Aradus enjoyed walking and taking in the sights of the city. It reminded him strongly of Rome. It also pleased him to see so many of his own people about. There were beautiful women in brightly colored stoles, elegant men wearing purple-trimmed white togas. There were so many legionnaires and officers about that Aradus felt he must be quite invisible. He relaxed a little.

As a major seaport, Caesarea had a steady influx of all nationalities. Aradus watched with interest the African and Arabian traders, the Damascene silk merchants.

Of course the Jews were here too. They seemed different, though. They didn't cross to the other side of the street when the Romans approached, as they did in Jerusalem. They would walk right past them, some even nodding at Cornelius. It was amazing.

It caused Aradus to study the man beside him. While he was short, he was powerfully built, almost like a Greek wrestler. He walked very erect with his hands clasped behind his back. From what Aradus could see from under the man's helmet, his hair was already white, though Cornelius wasn't much past forty-five.

His attractive eyes offset his large, flat nose and thin lips. Few people could agree on whether he was handsome or plain.

As Cornelius sensed Aradus relaxing, he pointed out various sights that he thought might interest him. He was careful not to ask any questions that would raise his guard again.

After filing down a few more streets, they came to the Temple of Augustus. It was truly an impressive sight. Like most Roman temples it was meant to inspire overpowering awe. It could not be seen properly without craning one's neck back to see the huge columns reaching to the sky. A large gilded pediment capped the Corinthian columns in front, while the attached columns along the sides supported the gracefully slanted roof. The entire temple rested on a huge base of massive stairs.

Though not religious, Aradus thought he wouldn't mind offering sacrifices there, just to stave off homesickness. After finding a place to tie up his horse, Aradus and Cornelius began the ascent up the temple steps. Despite the climb, Aradus felt renewed. The sea breeze was blowing over them and he was back among his own people. It reminded him of the far happier times of his boyhood, when the whole family would go to sacrifice at the local temple.

"I can almost imagine I'm home again," he said softly as they gained the top stair and turned to look back at the city.

Cornelius was wise enough to keep silent. He waited until the younger man had looked his fill before he led him to the temple priests.

The priests were full of plans for Aradus and the shields. This unexpected boon from the emperor had greatly enhanced their stature. To have this centurion especially assigned to the detail, they looked upon as another compliment from Rome.

Aradus quickly realized the priests were totally ignorant of the political ramifications that had brought the golden shields to their doorstep. He allowed himself to relax just a little more. Yes, he would certainly offer a sacrifice here.

After much exclamation on the beauty and costliness of the engraved shields, they began to discuss the best time for the dedication. Some wanted it to take place on the next feast day while two maintained that nothing would do but to wait for the annual Saturnalia festival. This set the rest of the temple priests howling at having to wait for nearly three and a half months before they could dedicate the shields.

Aradus watched in dismay as the group of priests argued on and on. He feared they would be at it all day. Whatever help Cornelius was supposed to offer him, he wasn't doing it now. He had backed into an alcove as if he wanted as little to do with the business as possible.

The sacred colleges of priests had impressive political and social powers, especially those priests connected with the pontifex maximus, the emperor as spiritual head. Only a fool would show them disrespect.

Coughing loudly, Aradus was finally able to make them stop and look at him. He bowed deeply before he spoke. "Sirs, I know such great matters must be discussed at length. Let me assure you that I will be at your disposal until the Jews' next Passover. I will be stationed here to oversee any orders that you may care to give. Please don't feel any constraints of time on your decisions."

Smiles broke out all around. The priests' vanity had been further petted, and Cornelius was amused at such a lengthy speech from the taciturn young man.

An old priest whose robes fit snugly over his fat paunch, came forward rubbing his hands. "Yes, yes. That's excellent. This will give us time to examine the entrails and take the auspices. Centurion, you may go now. We shall summon you when all the omens are properly read."

Mystified but pleased, Aradus bowed again. Cornelius joined him as he left the temple. The two men didn't stop until they had descended the steps and entered the courtyard.

Cornelius looked up at Aradus, a decided twinkle in his eyes. "Might I say, you handled the priests very well."

Aradus rubbed the back of his neck for a moment, then allowed a smile to lift one corner of his mouth. "Well, I didn't want to be there all day."

Cornelius paused for a moment then said, "Since you have completed the first day's assignment so well, you must join me in a close inspection of the public baths. They are just around the corner."

Aradus was surprised by the friendly invitation. He hesitated, not able to think of any plausible excuse. He would much rather have gone alone, but he saw no need to offend this man. Feeling very awkward, he nodded. "Yes."

Unfazed, Cornelius smiled and led the way down the crowded street.

CHAPTER ELEVEN

As the two men rounded a corner, Aradus saw a great rectangular building whose facade was honeycombed with arches. Each arch was either a doorway or held a small shop. There was a great deal of activity all about the place. People were buying and selling or passing through the doorways.

Cornelius led Aradus through one of the doorways and into the complex. Just a few steps within there was a notable change in the temperature. Cool, moist air greeted the two men. Cornelius looked up at Aradus and grinned.

A vaulted ceiling rose high above the tiled floor. Statues of various gods and goddesses lined the walls. The interior was divided in half. Two huge enclosures were built on either side of the spacious floor. Cornelius walked to the one on the right, Aradus following. This was the dressing room, a large area where one prepared for the baths. Slaves and servants were everywhere in attendance.

Cornelius, eager to get to the water, quickly removed his helmet, revealing a very smooth, bald head. His white hair only fringed the sides.

Aradus removed his helmet with greater reluctance, avoiding eye contact until he was sure Cornelius had his first glimpse. Any reaction Cornelius might have had he concealed well. He made it his business to get ready for the baths.

Neither man spoke again until both were up to their chins in water. Cornelius was a picture of tranquillity, his head resting against the side of the pool. Even Aradus wasn't scowling as much as usual.

Aradus decided Cornelius was an easy man to be around. He was friendly without talking too much. Several men in the large pool had greeted him. He had only smiled slowly and waved a languid hand as if not wishing to disturb the waters too much.

Most had nodded at Aradus. They were too well bred to stare, but he knew his strange, rough features had invoked curiosity.

After a quarter hour of silence, Cornelius moved a little closer. "You seemed a bit baffled when the priests talked of entrails and taking the auspices," he commented in his deep voice.

Aradus nodded. "I knew they examined sheep guts to tell the future, but I haven't heard of the auspices."

A broad smile lit the older man's face. "They claim they can tell the future by the way the sacred chickens eat."

"Sacred chickens?"

"Yes. The colleges of priests all have flocks of chickens at the temples. When they take the auspices, they watch the pattern of the chickens' eating in order to tell the future."

Aradus grimaced and shook his head.

Cornelius smiled again and continued to talk in his calm, resonant voice. "During the Punic Wars, they say Claudius

Pulcher took a whole flock of chickens aboard his ship in order to plan his battle strategies. The wretched birds became seasick and refused to eat at all. Furious, Pulcher threw the whole lot overboard, screaming, 'Then drink, if you won't eat!'"

Aradus nearly laughed. He tilted his head backward letting the water soak his short curls. When he looked forward again, he saw that Cornelius was studying him. Aradus sighed, aware of the distance his face always put between him and others. Irritated, he looked at the other centurion. "Curious?" he asked harshly.

Cornelius calmly cupped his hands in the water and bathed his own bald head. Only after rubbing his eyes did he answer. "Not really," he said, shrugging.

It was not the response Aradus had been expecting. His surprise caused him to lower his defenses just a bit. "I've been stared at so much, I've become oversensitive."

Cornelius sensed this was a rare admission. He nodded. "That's understandable."

Aradus would never know if it was the relaxing waters or the older man's calm acceptance. Perhaps it was a combination of both. Something deep within him let go and he began to talk of his injuries. Not how they had happened, for he had told that many times, but why they had happened. "A friend and I were in the same company. I was the standard bearer."

"A great honor."

"Yes, if anything, my friend Anthony was prouder of the honor than I. It meant a great deal to us, especially since we had both been placed in what we considered to be a poor unit.

"At any rate, we had been ordered on a campaign through the northern provinces as a show of strength, to put down any revolts. The campaign was doomed from the start. Supposedly all the omens had been wrong, but it was more a matter of poor leadership and bad planning. Anthony always rode directly behind me, swearing that if anything happened to me, he would grab the standard's pole before it ever hit the ground.

"A month into the campaign, as we arrived in Gaul, I spotted a movement ahead in the trees. It was an archer. Knowing the importance we Romans placed on our company standards, his arrow was trained on it instead of me. I swung to the side, protecting the standard. As I did so, I suddenly felt a white-hot burning along the side of my face as the arrow grazed me."

"But you saved the company standard?" Cornelius asked.

"Yes, and left my friend to take the arrow," he answered bleakly.

"It was a short and violent skirmish. We routed them completely, but in the melee they took Anthony's body to dishonor him. We never found him."

Aradus's eyes were unfocused. A lifetime of painful memories swam on their surfaces. "Many of us were badly wounded, but there were months of the campaign left. The men weren't the best to start with, and now they were disheartened.

"We boarded two ships at the northern coast of Gaul and sailed for Britain. We thought we had found a secluded beach to land on. When all but the ships' crews had come ashore we headed toward the woods. That's when we first saw them. Stepping from behind the trees was a dense array of armed warriors. Between them, women dressed in black ran back and forth, waving lit torches. All around, their priests began to scream hexes and incantations."

Aradus began to speak lower, ashamed of the story. "The superstitious fools in my company were terrified. They treated the ambushers as if they were ghosts, running before them like scared children."

"But you stood your ground," Cornelius said with quiet confidence.

Aradus brought his anguished eyes back to Cornelius. "Yes. Yes, I did. I barely had time to mount my horse before they were upon me. It was hard to fight surrounded as I was, with one hand clutching the standard pole."

"You never dropped it?"

"Never. How could I when Anthony had died for it?" Aradus asked simply.

"I heard an awful scream, just like an animal would make. I only remember what seemed to be a great bearlike man coming toward me with a club. He must have been incredible. They later found my helmet split in two.

"My last thought was for the standard. I was hit in such a way that I was thrust against the horse's neck. The standard was wedged between my body and the horse. Before I lost consciousness I clung to the horse's mane with all my might. Leaving me for dead, the barbarians decided to finish off the rest of the men before claiming my horse.

"The sailors on the ships had watched all this in horror, before rousing themselves to rescue us. They freed all the galley slaves below deck and were able to muster enough force to take the beach for a short while. Many of our men had turned coward and had run screaming to the woods. The ships' captains ordered them to be stranded there as their just reward."

Cornelius watched the younger man's face, enthralled by his tale.

"I'm told at that point, two sailors were carrying our

wounded lieutenant to the boats when he saw me. He ordered them to set him down and reclaim the company standard. They tried to do as they were bid, but the horse bolted, carrying me and the standard into the woods.

"There was no help for it. The Britons were recovering, so all our people had to retreat to the ships. The lieutenant was beside himself. His men had disgraced him, and now the standard was lost. He vowed they would never return to Rome without it. He would have taken his life if he hadn't been too wounded to do it.

"For three days the ships sailed as close to shore as they dared. At night men would swim to the beach, hoping to find the last tangible piece of pride the company had.

"They say on the third night close to dawn, a man spotted my horse. He was surprised to see me still lying across the beast, the standard safely protected. He had no trouble approaching the exhausted horse. It came eagerly forward, wanting to rid itself of the heavy burden it had born for so long. Amazed, the man found my body was still warm and pliable, though he had to cut the horse's mane from my clenched fingers. With great difficulty, he brought me and the standard back to the ship."

"Incredible," Cornelius murmured. "How could you recover from such a wound?"

"It took a very long time. I knew nothing of the journey back, though the lieutenant in his gratitude saw that I received the best of care. Even after I came to, I stammered like an imbecile for a month or more."

"You are a hero."

Aradus shrugged as he settled back into the water. He tipped his head back and closed his eyes. "Others thought so too. I was honored at the same ceremony which decimated what remained of my unit."

"Decimated," Cornelius repeated softly.

"Yes. With great pomp my unit was lined up before me and every tenth man killed. They then wiped every mention of our company's name from existence."

"The lieutenant thanked me for my efforts, then promptly went out and killed himself."

Aradus let his arms float at his sides, as relaxed as he could ever remember being. He finished his story. "Honored I was, but there was still the shadow of my ill-fated unit that I couldn't escape. Not to mention my face. It began to be rumored that I had somehow deserved my wounds. That I was so ill-favored because of the gods' displeasure. I was avoided by everyone.

"My family had enough influence to see that I got the promotion the lieutenant had promised me. They also arranged for me to be transferred as far from Rome as possible."

At the very back of his mind a voice whispered that he would regret saying so much to Cornelius. It was very easy to ignore, though. Relief washed over him, as cleansing as the waters.

With very little effort he could have fallen asleep right there in the baths, so relaxed was he. His tranquility smoothed out his features enough for Cornelius to trace what was once a very handsome face.

Cornelius watched him with seeming calmness, his bald head resting against the side of the pool. His eyes were nearly shut. He was far from sleep. He was praying. Cornelius, whose genealogy could be traced to Romulus and Remus, was praying to the God of the Jews, praying that He might have mercy on a bitter young man named Aradus.

CHAPTER TWELVE

After time spent at the baths, Cornelius brought Aradus to the barracks. The sea air blew a cool freshness through his new quarters, causing him to sleep soundly throughout the night.

When he arose the next morning he headed straight for the Temple of Augustus, to see if the priests had any orders for him. He had gone several streets when he noticed a small centurion coming out of a Jewish bookstall. Seeing it was Cornelius, he crossed over to meet him. He was slightly uneasy as he recalled all he had told this man about his past.

As Cornelius saw Aradus approaching he looked somewhat uneasy himself. He carried a large bucketlike canister often used to hold the scrolls of large books. He shifted the canister to his hip and offered a salute with his free hand.

Aradus returned the salute and greeted him. "Good morning."

"Aradus. I trust you slept well?"

"Like a stone."

"It's the sea air," Cornelius said smiling. "I sleep better

now than I did in Rome. So, where are you headed? The temple?"

"Yes. Perhaps the priests have had time to check the sacred chickens."

"I'll come along if you like. I've been instructed to offer you any assistance that will—"

Before he could finish, Cornelius was interrupted by the Jewish shopkeeper. He had stuck his shaggy head out of his stall and called to Cornelius in Aramaic.

Cornelius answered him in the same tongue with a flawless accent.

The Jew then said something while making a pushing motion with his two hands. Both the Jew and Cornelius laughed.

Still laughing Cornelius touched the other centurion on the shoulder and led him into the street. "Come. Zacharias fears the sight of two centurions in front of his shop will scare away all his customers."

Aradus looked back at the man and scowled. He felt the Jew was being far too familiar with Cornelius. He didn't understand how the centurion could encourage such impudent remarks from a Jew.

The two men walked in silence for a few streets. Then pointing to the canister Cornelius held, Aradus asked, "The Scriptures?"

Surprised, Cornelius looked up at Aradus then held the heavy canister out between his two large hands. "Yes. Zacharias had just received a translation I could read. I can speak Aramaic rather well, but I've never mastered reading Hebrew. Have you read the Scriptures?"

"Only parts and in Greek. My uncle had a translation. My uncle is a great student of the Jews' literature. He is a wise man, but I fear he has been among the Jews too long."

Cornelius only smiled at the thinly cloaked rebuke. He had not missed Aradus's reaction to his exchange with Zacharias. "Do you fear your uncle might be proselytized by the Jews and become a worshiper of their God?"

Aradus stopped in the street, staring at Cornelius. "Lyconides?" he snorted. "Never!"

Having hit his mark, Cornelius could barely refrain from laughing. He placed his hand on the young man's elbow to start him walking again. "No offense meant, Aradus. It has happened, you know. Perfectly sound Romans far from home, seduced by some evil pagan religion."

It was well that Aradus couldn't see the amusement dancing in Cornelius's eyes. As it was, the young man nodded in agreement. "Yes, I've seen . . . a few cases of that myself. People can be so gullible. Now there's this Jew named Jesus going about. A few lucky coincidences occur and He has a following."

"I've heard the stories. Have you seen Him?" Cornelius asked eagerly.

"Yes," he answered shortly. "In Capernaum."

Cornelius was full of questions but he hesitated, noting that Aradus had stopped again and was staring straight ahead. Following his gaze, Cornelius saw that he was staring at the small entourage winding its way to the temple.

Recovering himself, Aradus turned to his companion. In as neutral a voice as possible, he asked, "Those ensigns on the litters, don't they belong to Pilate?"

"Hmm? Oh yes. Notice the gold embossing? Only the finest for the governor."

Aradus digested this, then commented, "I never dreamed Pilate was so devout as to offer sacrifices this early in the morning."

Cornelius rolled his eyes then shook his head. "Heavens

no, man. Pilate will still be among his silken pillows at this hour. That must be his wife, Procla. She is very devout, or very superstitious, depending upon how you look at it. Her life is totally ruled by portents and omens."

"I see."

Cornelius shifted the canister to his other hip. Using his free hand he began to rub his chin thoughtfully. After a moment of concentration, he turned his warm amber eyes to Aradus. "Aradus, as the gilded shields were a major source of embarrassment to Pilate, perhaps we should come back when his wife has left."

Confounded, the young man slowly turned to face Cornelius. "What do you know about the shields?"

"Only what all of Palestine knows. Pilate tried to force Roman symbols down the Jews' throats and ended up getting them rammed down his own." Cornelius lowered his voice, "I don't have to tell you how unpopular the man is. He's gone out of his way to antagonize these people since he came here. Any mortification he suffers is going to be the news of the day."

"True."

"The college of priests are probably the only ones who still think the shields were originally meant for the Temple of Augustus. But who's going to tell them otherwise? Not Pilate, that's for sure. He's going to have to put the best face on this dedication as possible, even if it means personally attending the ceremonies. Though I'm sure he's bellowing like a stuck pig in the privacy of his chambers."

The whole business seemed to amuse Cornelius, but Aradus felt worse than he had in days. He hadn't dreamed Pilate's humiliation would be so universally known. The man must be beside himself. As Cornelius had said nothing about any traitorous centurions, he could only hope that part was still not commonly known in Caesarea.

The two men watched in silence as the entourage ascended the temple steps. When they finally went in, Cornelius turned to Aradus. "I think a tour of the city is in order. Something that would take a few hours. Don't you agree?"

Aradus nodded, glad to be leaving the temple and the closeness of anyone related to Pilate.

Cornelius was an intelligent and thoughtful guide. He showed Aradus only those things he thought would interest him. He purposely avoided the amphitheater. Fearful that Aradus might want to go in and see that day's spectacle, he made a long, circuitous route around it. He needn't have worried, though Aradus had never had a taste for any of the blood-letting events that passed for entertainment. Cornelius ended his tour with the artificial harbor that had allowed Caesarea to become a great seaport.

As the two men stood on the concrete wall overlooking the sea, Aradus found himself envying the man beside him. He had been right: Cornelius was a very easy man to be around. He used his beautifully modulated voice sparingly, engaging in conversation only when necessary. Yet at all times he projected a warm acceptance of whomever he was with. The man was a born listener. His personality seemed to force the most reticent of men into making confidences.

"You're a lucky man, Cornelius. Stationed in a Roman city, surrounded by Romans."

Cornelius folded his powerful arms across his chest and looked out to sea. He searched within himself for the right words, words that could reach this man. "I am very . . . blessed, Aradus. I'm at peace with myself and my surroundings. Yet I think I can say without boasting, I would have this peace whether I was stationed here or in Jerusalem."

Aradus looked at the man standing so calmly there

beside him. He knew what he was saying was true. He then turned his gaze to a small ship just coming into the harbor. "Peace," he said. "That is something I have never known."

CHAPTER THIRTEEN

As the two men stood watching the ship coming into the harbor, they became aware of the measured cadence of footsteps on the paved street behind them. Turning, they saw two guards coming towards them.

"Humph," Cornelius grunted. "Pilate's guards. I wonder what the soft puppies want?"

Aradus felt a great coldness start to spread through his stomach as the two soldiers approached. They were a pair of very young men, probably picked for their exalted duty because of important relations rather than merit. They stopped with a sharp precision before the two older men.

After executing their salutes, the one on the right addressed Cornelius, though both were looking at Aradus. "Centurion."

"Yes?"

"This centurion," he jerked his head toward Aradus, "he's just arrived from Jerusalem?"

Amused at the youth's officiousness, Cornelius turned

playfully to Aradus. "Centurion," he mimicked the guard, "are you just arrived from Jerusalem?"

Ignoring Cornelius, Aradus glowered at the young men. "Who wants to know?"

Enraged at not being taken seriously, both guards turned red, while the first one spluttered, "Governor Pilate! Now are you from Jerusalem or not?"

Cornelius already knew Aradus's bad temper, so he held up a conciliatory hand. "Now, now. Yes, he's from Jerusalem. Why don't you just state your business with him."

Not liking the older man's fatherly tone, the young men were further incensed. The spokesman for the two looked as if he were ready to stomp his foot in anger. Aradus was suddenly reminded of another boy he had infuriated—little Guni, so many miles away. The thought unaccountably softened him towards this young man.

"Does the governor wish to see me?" Aradus asked in an altered tone.

"Yes. Immediately."

"Then of course I will obey." He turned to Cornelius, resigned to whatever fate had in store. He wanted to take leave of the older man, certain he would never see him again. He was glad now he had unburdened himself to him. "Cornelius?"

"Yes?"

Aradus frowned not sure what to say. In a very uncharacteristic move, Aradus placed his hand on the man's shoulder. "Perhaps I will find peace after all."

Puzzled, Cornelius only nodded, then watched the three men walk away. He could not know that the peace Aradus was referring to was his death.

After the men arrived at the governor's palace, they led Aradus through a labyrinth of beautifully decorated hallways. He was finally brought to a awning-covered balcony that faced the sea. Pilate and his wife were there, reclining on two couches covered with red silk. Slaves were aiding the slight breeze by waving ostrich feather fans.

Out of respect, Aradus had removed his helmet as soon as he had entered the palace. Upon entering the balcony his poor face had effected the usual responses. Procla was ruder than most women he had met. She curled her painted lip and raised her heavily ringed hand to her chest in disgust.

Governor Pilate regarded him through half-lidded eyes, as if considering something. He was a tall, thin man consumed with nervous energy. Even as he reclined on the couch he would tap a foot or drum his fingers on the gold-embroidered satin. He was going to some lengths to pretend indifference to Aradus's appearance. He had wanted this interview badly, but he didn't wish to show it.

Procla had no such compunction. A small birdlike woman, she had watched Aradus avidly from the moment he came in. She sat straight up, plucking a cluster of grapes from the table between the couches. She was the type of woman who always needed something to do, at least to have something in her hands. She began to pull the grapes apart as she waited for her husband to speak.

Resting his weight on his right elbow, Pilate made a show of examining the nails on his left hand. Finally he deigned to speak. "Ah, centurion, I hear you are freshly arrived from Jerusalem."

"Yes, sir."

"You were ordered to oversee the shields' dedication?"

"Yes, sir."

Pilate swung his feet to the tiled floor and stood up. He was even taller than Aradus, though he weighed far less. He stood quite still while the air moved about his long, white toga. He reminded Aradus of a bird of prey. "There are not enough centurions in Caesarea, that they must be shipped in from Jerusalem?" Suspicion weighed his voice down.

Aradus was not sure how to answer. He looked into Pilate's eyes. "I . . . I follow my orders, sir."

"Do you? Always?"

"Yes, sir."

Pilate walked to the edge of the balcony and laid a hand on the balustrade. In a quick motion, his wife joined him. She stared hard at Aradus then looked up at her tall husband. "My lord, no one could forget a face like that! If this were the man—"

"Quiet, woman," Pilate commanded in irritation. He turned at the sound of someone entering. Another guard had come. Aradus was sure he had come for him. But Pilate seemed annoyed at his presence. "What is it?" he asked with asperity.

"My lord, the head priest of the temple wishes an audience."

"Not now!"

Afraid, Procla clutched at his arm. "My lord," she whispered urgently. "We must not offend the man!"

More annoyed than ever, Pilate shook her hand from his arm. "You're right, but for all the wrong reasons. I fear the man's politics more than his prophecies." Addressing the guard, he said, "Show the priest in."

Pilate stared balefully at Aradus while they waited for the priest, the centurion trying to look as innocuous as his nature would allow.

The priest entered, wreathed in smiles. He made a respectful bow to Pilate, then seeing Aradus, he gave the centurion a hearty clap on the back. "My lord, I had come to thank you for your kind attentions to the temple, and what do I find? Here you are conferring with the excellent fellow chosen to oversee the dedication. If only all our officials were as piously conscientious as you!"

Pilate smiled weakly.

"Believe me, sir. I will not forget your thoughtfulness, nor will the rest of the college of priests."

Pilate made a polite nod.

"In fact I wanted you to be the first to know, that after careful consultations, all omens point to the great Saturnalia festival as being the best time for the dedication. That is especially fortuitous as we all know you are always in Caesarea at that time to preside over the festival. It's so good to know you will be there to receive the acknowledgment you deserve."

Aradus held his breath. Pilate would either explode at the man's stupidity or go along with the charade. If the priest's regard was important enough to Pilate, Aradus might be safe, as he was a part of the dedication.

After what seemed to be a lifetime, Pilate finally spoke. "Anything that honors the Temple of Augustus honors Caesar, which is, of course, what we all want. Please let me know if I can be of any further help."

Aradus began breathing again.

"Well, if you are done with this young man," the fat priest pointed to Aradus, "I did have some business to discuss with him."

Forcing himself to look at Pilate, Aradus was relieved to see the governor had lost some of the fire in his eyes.

"Yes, of course. I have no further need of him."

As Aradus followed the priest out of the palace he was so relieved he even offered up a prayer to any god that might be listening. Little did he know that Cornelius was doing a very similar thing in another part of the city.

CHAPTER FOURTEEN

The temple priest walking with Aradus was blithely unaware of the maelstrom of emotions going through the centurion. While the priest prattled on about ceremonies and rituals, Aradus was examining himself.

He had truly believed he was going to die, and perhaps even be tortured first as a vent to Pilate's rage and humiliation. Then being reprieved so easily had left him shaken. He had faced death many times before in battle. But it was one thing when one's blood was up for the fight, and quite another when one had to wait for a man to drop the axe.

Aradus was surprised at how badly he wanted to live. Why? His life was a hard one. His duties had become onerous. He had no one he cared for. Yet there was something in him that desperately wanted to survive.

It really was an incredible thing that the priest had come just at the time Pilate was examining him. The man's presence had saved his life. It was one of those lucky coincidences he had been discussing with Cornelius. Or was it?

Had some long-absent god finally decided to intervene on his behalf? Aradus considered this thought for a long moment, then shook his head in dissent.

The priest beside him stopped, looking flustered. "You disagree?" he demanded.

Aradus broke from his reverie, realizing he had somehow managed to irritate the priest. "What, sir?"

"I was discussing the proper observance of the Saturnalia ceremony and you shook your head. Just what do you disagree with?"

"I really must be honest with you, sir, I was thinking of something else."

"Oh?" the man was instantly offended.

"Yes. I was thinking what an oaf I was. Here you are, an important man known throughout the city, and I have yet to learn your name. I hope you can forgive such boorish ignorance."

The priest was satisfied. As long as the centurion gave him his proper respect, he could overlook such minor lapses. "Ah well, you are just arrived from the backwaters. Tychicus, my name is Lucius Tychicus Apuleius," he said importantly.

"Thank you."

The two men then continued on to the temple, Aradus attending very closely to everything Tychicus said.

As the weeks passed Aradus was kept very busy. His duties were not hard, but extremely detailed. The priests were quite exacting in what they wanted done.

He worked closely with Cornelius as it was his men who would be doing all the dirty work. They also would be employed to keep some semblance of order when the days of the carnival arrived.

It had not taken him long to see how vastly different Cornelius was from any other officer he had known. He used his authority as lightly as it was possible and still maintained discipline. He took a fatherly concern for all his men, noting if any had problems. He would even leave his door open in the evening in case some man needed counseling.

Despite his friendliness, Aradus noted that Cornelius would not frequent the many places where the other officers socialized. Caesarea was full of possibilities for any soldier with enough money. But of all the establishments that Aradus became familiar with during his stay in the city, he never once met Cornelius there.

Shortly before the Saturnalia, there was a night when Aradus had stayed out much later than usual. The day had been a long one. He had become weary with being an errand boy for the priests and had imbibed far more than was his wont.

Aradus had never been a happy, sloppy drunk as so many of the other soldiers were. Instead he would become quieter and angrier as the wine did its work. His ugly face would take on a vicious cast as he brooded on every wrong ever done to him. He probably would have killed when he got in such a state, but the very sight of his malevolent appearance made everyone stay far out of his reach.

So it was that night that, as Aradus stormed back to the barracks, all the other soldiers avoided him. All except one.

Aradus had been quartered near Cornelius. He had to go past the man's door to reach his own. As usual, Cornelius had left the door open while he talked to two young soldiers who had been having differences. One of the youths had decided to leave early. He had the great misfortune of walking out the door when Aradus tried to walk past. The two men collided.

With a bellow of rage, Aradus struck the young man

across the mouth, sending him reeling. Before the youth could hit the ground, Aradus grabbed him with his left hand, then slammed into his stomach with his right fist. Aradus went to hit him again, but something had pinned back his right arm. Furious, Aradus whipped around to see Cornelius holding his arm.

"Let me go, little man!" Aradus rasped through clenched teeth.

Cornelius only answer was to yank his arm back up to his shoulder blades. Drunk as he was, Aradus knew that this most effective hold could break his arm if he resisted further. Looking into the blazing eye of Cornelius, he judged the normally mild man wouldn't hesitate to break it in two or three places if he had to.

Swearing, Aradus dropped the youth to the ground. Other soldiers had appeared, circling them. They looked to Cornelius for orders.

He nodded at three of them. "Take Statius to the infirmary."

Cornelius then turned back to Aradus. His deep voice was charged with emotions of anger and remorse. "I should break both your arms, then wrap them in chains! Do I have to? Or will you scrape up enough dignity to go with these men like an officer?"

Aradus weaved unsteadily on his feet, considering. The pain of his arm was sobering him fast. He looked at Cornelius with a hatred he didn't feel, then grunted. "I'll go, I'll go."

Cornelius gave his arm another small yank as a reminder, then slowly released his iron grip. He waited a moment, in case Aradus resisted, then nodded to the remaining four soldiers.

"Escort him to his quarters. If he tries anything, anything

at all, chain him to his bed."

Without a backward glance, Cornelius left for the infirmary.

The next morning Aradus awoke to a raging headache. He moaned softly and rolled away from the wall he had pressed against all night as he slept on the floor. It was a few groggy moments before he realized he was not alone. Cornelius was standing over him, a picture of displeasure.

Surprised, Aradus wondered what Cornelius was doing. He also wondered why he was lying flat on his back on the hard floor. Too soon, the memories of last night came flooding in, filling him with shame.

He slowly got up, his head throbbing all the while. He made his way across the room and sat down heavily on the bed. He waited for Cornelius to speak.

Cornelius was silent.

Aradus knew his behavior had been inexcusable. He had behaved like one of the barbarians. He had badly beaten a young man and insulted another man he deeply respected. He had been wronged so often in his life, he couldn't believe he now held the role of antagonist.

Despite his remorse, his defenses were up. His shame was twisting, making him sullen. After a few more moments of continued silence, he frowned at Cornelius. "Go on, then, let's hear it."

"You broke the boy's jaw. They can't fix it. He'll be disfigured for life."

A wave of horror broke over Aradus. No, no, he would never inflict on another man what he'd been forced to endure. He hardly ever got drunk, just one night, and he'd ruined another man's life.

Cornelius didn't understand Aradus's silence. He misinterpreted it completely. Filled with frustrated sorrow, his normally strong reserves broke and he began to berate the man. "I've tried to work with you, show you friendship. This is how you repay me? By destroying the career of one of my men? We'll have to send him home; he's in too much pain to soldier."

Aradus looked stonily at the floor.

"Doesn't that bother you? You, of all people, should know what's in store for this young man."

Aradus winced, knowing too well.

Cornelius looked at the brooding hulk before him. He thought of all the hours of prayer he had spent for this man. He couldn't understand it. Aradus had become worse, not better.

"Despite your self-pity, you are a lucky man. You couldn't have picked a better victim. Statius is an orphan with no high-born kinsmen to come after you. You also picked your time well. With the Saturnalia and the shield dedication next week, I'm sure that Pilate and the priests will force our legate here to wink at your despicable behavior. In fact, he's not even mentioned it, though it's been noised throughout the barracks."

Disgusted that Aradus would make no reply, Cornelius walked to the door. Putting his hand on the latch, he turned back to Aradus. "If you wanted to be avenged for your sorrows, you have done that. Still, I hope . . . I want to believe that you are truly repentant for what you have done to him."

Aradus couldn't have been sorrier, but his infernal pride kept his mouth tightly shut.

An insurmountable gulf lay between the two men as Cornelius walked out the door.

CHAPTER FIFTEEN

The Roman people carefully observed a religious calendar that was full of fasti and nefasti days (days where public business was permitted or forbidden). They also observed great annual festivals. The most animated of these was the great Saturnalia held in December, a carnival that had once been part of the rustic celebrations that ended the fall planting. At the Saturnalia slaves were given temporary freedoms and were served by their masters. The Romans would exchange gifts such as small dolls and wax candles. The revelries were completed when a mock king was crowned.

As it was still very much a religious holiday, it was the perfect time to dedicate the gilded shields at the temple. At the height of the festivities, the beautiful shields were brought up to the temple and officially consigned to the care of the priests. In their most ornate robes, the priests performed a complicated liturgy to dedicate the shields to the service of Rome's spiritual head, Caesar.

Pilate and his wife were there occupying seats of honor.

While Procla looked properly reverent, Pilate looked as if he were suffering from a sour stomach. At rapt attention on either side were two centurions, Aradus and Cornelius. Aradus was fighting boredom, and Cornelius was silently praying that Jehovah would forgive him for his presence at such unholy activities.

After two hours of mind-numbing rituals the shields were properly dedicated and hung in places of honor. Light reflected off their intricately carved surfaces, greatly brightening the interior of the temple.

Aradus, along with Pilate, hoped he would never see the wretched things again. Cornelius and he flanked the governor and his wife as they left the temple. After they had escorted the pair to their litters, they waited respectfully in the street while the entourage made its sedate passage back to the palace.

After the small parade was gone, Cornelius turned to Aradus. They had not spoken in days. Cornelius had forgiven him, but he truly did not know what to say. Aradus, assuming he had lost the man's regard forever, had kept a proud silence.

"Well, your job here is done," Cornelius commented in a disinterested tone.

It was true, but Livius had made it clear Aradus was not to return for another two and a half months, until the Passover week. Aradus realized for the first time what an awkward position that put him in. He couldn't leave Caesarea, but he had no real duties to perform.

He looked down at Cornelius, wondering how he could spend another day at the barracks where he was so openly despised, let alone ten weeks. Livius, seventy miles away, was still playing havoc with his life.

Once again Cornelius misinterpreted Aradus's silence. Thinking Aradus a lost cause, he turned to go. Before he left he said over his shoulder, "Clear your quarters out, then; we could use the space."

"I can't leave," he replied gruffly.

"What?" Cornelius turned back.

"My legate gave me orders not to return until the Jews' Passover week."

Cornelius put his hands on his hips and looked up at Aradus suspiciously. "Whatever for?"

Irritated by his situation and Cornelius's obvious desire to see him gone, Aradus shrugged and answered roughly, "Those are my orders. I don't have to explain them to you."

"No, but you will have to explain to my legate. Believe me, he'll want to know what you're hanging about for."

"Don't worry, I'll talk to him." Not that he had any idea what he'd say. It did not seem appropriate to respond that his legate was using him as a scapegoat.

Cornelius bit back an angry retort. It was beneath them to wrangle like two fishmongers in the street. "The legate is at camp and in a rare good mood, owing no doubt to the week's festivities. I would strongly suggest your not waiting to spring your news on him. You should know by now you're not exactly a welcomed guest at the barracks."

"I know it."

Cornelius stared at the ground, hating to be at odds with anyone, especially a man he had so wanted to help. He prayed for the wisdom to touch a heart more deformed than Aradus's face. "Aradus," he said in a low voice. "You and I . . . we're Romans. We're bred to be fighters, raised to be harsh. We go to the amphitheater to watch animals rend men to bits and call it entertainment. We go to theaters where men are actually executed on stage just to make a play more realistic. Violence is our meat and drink, yet we call those we subdue the barbarians."

Aradus frowned at Cornelius, not sure of his point.

The older man was frustrated, not sure of what to say. "Some of these so-called barbarians could teach us. Teach us about the worth of a man, teach us about peace."

"You sound like my uncle," Aradus grated. "They could not defend themselves from subjugation, but you would make them out to be something wonderful."

"No, Aradus, they are not wonderful. It is their faith and beliefs that are wonderful."

Despite his irritation, Aradus was touched that Cornelius would bother to speak with him. It was a consideration he had not expected. "Cornelius . . . I do not love violence for its own sake." He paused, then looked the man in the eye. "I would give all the gold in the empire to make Statius whole again. But prattling on the very steps of Caesar's temple about the virtue of the Jews is not going to do either one of us any good."

"True enough. Would you like me to take you to the legate now?"

"Yes, I might as well deal with him and get it over with."

The legate of Caesarea, Propertius Lucan, had very pleasant quarters overlooking the harbor. When Cornelius and Aradus arrived and were shown into the rooms, they saw that Lucan had been conferring with one of his lieutenants.

Propertius Lucan was a man in his sixties. Never brilliant, but always well connected, he had made a slow but steady rise to his present rank. He had made life easy for himself and his many powerful friends. He was generally regarded as a charming, obliging man—honest when it was convenient, loyal as long as it was safe.

He liked everything to run as smoothly as possible. He detested difficulties and complications. He saw to it that his officers were efficient men who would not bother him with a lot of problems.

He had labeled Aradus as a problem over a week ago, a problem he wanted long gone. He looked up with disgust to see the man coming towards him.

Lucan dropped the scroll he was holding to a nearby table. He placed his thick, stubby hands on his broad stomach, then looked down his nose at Aradus. "Yes?" he asked with asperity.

This was not a promising start.

Aradus saluted but the legate did not bother to return it. "Sir, I felt I should explain my orders to you."

"What's to explain? The shields are dedicated; you can go back to Jerusalem now."

"Sir, my legate stipulated I was not to return until the Passover week."

"What? You have no more duties here."

"I know, sir."

Lucan paused, then looking at Cornelius and the lieutenant, he said, "The two of you will excuse us for a moment."

He waited until the two had left before he spoke again. "I have dealt with Marcus Livius before. He is a man who does nothing without a very good reason. I have also found it is usually better not to know what his reasons are. Perhaps he just wants to be rid of you for a time. After your disgraceful behavior I can understand that. Perhaps he has other, deeper reasons." Lucan was well aware that a centurion had tipped off the Jews to the shields, thus precipitating their being sent to Caesarea. "Still, what am I to do with you?"

Lucan's first thought was to confine him to quarters for two and a half months, but that might cause more problems than it solved. He didn't want the temple priests to know he had imprisoned their pet. "Cornelius!" he finally called out. The centurion immediately reentered. "Sir?"

"He's all yours for the next ten weeks. Keep him sober and out of trouble. Keep him away from me. Just . . . I don't know, share your duty roster with him."

Burning with shame, Aradus left the legate with Cornelius in tow. One night's lapse, one awful night, and he had been branded as a drunk and a troublemaker.

Aradus could not believe how slowly the weeks passed. Each day dragged on forever, while he was forced to endure the hateful gazes of the soldiers. Statius had been very popular. His fellow legionnaires were galled that the man who had caused him to be sent away was still among them.

Cornelius was aware of the purgatory Aradus was enduring; he often wondered if it would soften or harden him. Aradus kept his own counsel. After each day's work he would shut the door to his quarters and not come out again until the first light of morning.

Finally the time did pass, and Aradus was free to go. The morning he was to leave, Cornelius went to his quarters a good hour before the dawn, knowing the young centurion would leave at the first opportunity.

Aradus was surprised to hear a knock at his door, surprised to see Cornelius standing on the other side.

"You're already dressed, Aradus. Packed too, I see."

"Yes. I thought I'd please everyone by leaving at the first light."

Cornelius held a scroll in his hand. He held it towards Aradus. "There has been so much I wanted to say to you. I think this says it better than I could."

Aradus looked down at the scroll then back at Cornelius. "It's part of the Scriptures. That translation cost you dearly. I don't—"

Cornelius held up his hand. "Please, Aradus. I know my giving you this is more important to me than it is to you.

Will you take it? As a gesture of the friendship that might have been?"

Affected greatly by his words, Aradus took the scroll. "Yes. We could have been friends. I thank you that we do not part as enemies."

Cornelius stepped back and saluted. Aradus did the same. Then taking his pack and the scroll, he went to collect his horse. The prayers of Cornelius followed after him.

CHAPTER SIXTEEN

Aradus's return trip to Jerusalem was not the solitary journey his departure had been. The roads were clogged with Jews making their way to Jerusalem. They all wanted to celebrate the Passover in the holy city. The branch of highway leading from the sea was especially crowded, as the towns of Joppa and Lydda poured out their inhabitants.

Aradus was glad for the long legs of his horse. He was able to cut through the crowds with ease, while the majority of the Jews were forced to slog along on foot.

He had ridden for a few hours when his sharp eyes caught the glint of gold. Some of his fellow passengers down the road were very finely arrayed. He rode up a small knoll for a better view.

He stared intently down upon the sea of humanity until he found the brilliant gold fittings again. There to the left was a large ornate sedan and several riders.

Who would be so rich and so bold as to flaunt his wealth on the open road? Only a man wealthy and powerful enough to have personal guards. Aradus stared again, then swore by a few minor deities. It was Pilate down there, obviously making his way to Jerusalem.

Aradus leaned back in his saddle and looked at the sky. He cursed again. He wanted to charge his horse down the road, right past Pilate's long nose, and even offer a jaunty salute as he raced by. But he knew the far wiser course was to hang back, keeping plenty of distance between the governor and him.

Slowly dismounting, Aradus let out a long sigh. I must be getting old, he thought to himself. He hobbled his horse and went to sit in the shade of a large boulder. As he leaned his back against its cool surface, he thought of little Guni hiding behind a similar rock. He thought for a moment of the boy. He wished he was there now to talk to, even if he only wanted to talk about his strange friend, Jesus.

Aradus wondered at the interest this Jesus aroused. What kind of Jew was this, that even learned Romans such as his uncle and Cornelius would be interested in Him?

Thinking of Cornelius reminded him of the scroll he had been given. This would be as good a time as any to read it. Retrieving it from his pack, he settled back to read.

The writings he quickly found to be vastly different than what he had read before. These were written by specifically named men. The Book he was reading from now was by a man named Isaiah.

Aradus frowned to himself. This Isaiah said it was a vision. Now what in thunder was that supposed to mean? Was it a work of fiction? And what was this jumping around with tenses? Here it spoke of the past, there it spoke in the present, and there again it spoke of things to come. He shook his head in frustration.

His face became blank with surprise as he read on. Isaiah

had actually written about their God being angry with the Jews. He had not expected this. Isaiah had written about consequences and judgments for wrongdoing. Aradus had only expected self-serving platitudes. How real it all seemed. How honest.

The sun shifted and stole away his shade, but still Aradus read on. After their judgment the Jews were promised the hope of redemption. Hope—what a sweet thing Aradus knew it to be. It seemed hope was there for everyone: the hungry, the thirsty, even the barren.

Something twisted deep within Aradus; an unbidden longing shot through him. What about hope for a deformed, friendless Roman? Would any be offered to him?

He shoved the strange thought away and continued reading. Who was this Redeemer? In one breath, Isaiah seemed to speak of Him as God and as man. How could that be? Surely only a God could "[bear] the sin of many, and [make] intercession for the transgressors." Yet it spoke very clearly of His death and His grave. How could God die? Was this the Messiah he had heard that the Jews believed in?

Aradus mulled this over in his mind for a while. He was very confused. It seemed as if Isaiah spoke of a man who was God and a God who was man. How strange. Yet it was somehow comforting. A God who had lived as a man would understand a man. He would really know how difficult life could be. Aradus was especially touched by the part that said He had no form, no comeliness, no beauty. He had always been taught that the gods were images of perfection. Except the misshapen god Vulcan of course, and no one wanted to be like him.

Aradus snorted. What was he thinking? There was no God-man or anyone like that. Such a being could be no more real than the hapless Vulcan or his ilk.

Still, Aradus looked down and smoothed the parchment with a rare, gentle gesture. If there was a God, any type of God at all, wouldn't it be wonderful if He was like the one written of here?

Aradus carefully rolled the parchment, then placed it in its cylinder. He leaned his head back and looked to the sky. He thought for a moment how he would look from another point of view. What would a God think of an ugly, dirty Roman sitting in the dirt?

"He'd think I was a fool for sitting out in the sun!" he declared aloud to the sky. He scrambled to his feet and unhobbled his horse. Mounting, he peered down the road. He saw no hint of Pilate. He rode down the road and continued his journey.

The road from Emmaus led straight to Golgotha and on to Jerusalem. It was the most congested yet. People were actually forced to stand and wait before they could enter the city.

Hating the press of people, Aradus decided to ride south along the city wall and enter at the southern gate. He soon found the same situation of clogged pedestrian traffic.

Shrugging, he decided to try the southeastern gate. It was much wider than the other two. Surely he could get in there. As he drew closer to the southeastern gate he saw the same mass of people, but with a difference. They had made irregular columns along either side of the gate and were chanting something.

During his time in Judea, he had picked up very few Hebrew words. Greek was so commonly used by Jew and Gentile alike, there had never been any need to learn Aramaic or Hebrew. But he did know the word *hosanna*. It meant "save now." The people were saying it over and over. What did they want saving from? The Romans?

Concerned, he pressed in as closely as he could without

trampling anyone. His horse made it easy for him to see over the heads of the human columns. He was puzzled to see a tiny parade of thirteen men making their way to the gate between the rows of people. Only one man was riding. He was astride a white donkey with only garments for a saddle. He was the obvious focal point of all the excitement. People were waving palm branches at Him as if they were expensive feathered fans. They were throwing their own coats and jackets before the colt, making a cloth carpet for the beast's feet.

Aradus knew he had seen the man before, but he couldn't remember where. He could never tell one of these people from another. Suddenly an old crone of a woman began waving her skinny arms wildly and shouting, "Jesus! Jesus!"

Of course, Aradus thought, it's that Jew from Capernaum. He wondered if all this display was some religious parade or a show of political strength. Whatever it was, he was sure his superiors would want to know about it.

Once inside the gate, Jesus and His followers went due north, obviously intent upon going to the Temple. Aradus headed northwest, across the Valley of the Cheesemakers and the Essene quarter. Despite the crowds he made good time in getting to Herod's palace and the barracks.

He wasted no time in finding the legate, much as he loathed the man. Fortunately, Livius was in his quarters, with the door open to let in any slight breeze. Aradus stood on the threshold and saluted. "Sir."

Livius looked up from the couch where he was sitting reading a dispatch. His brows lifted over his beautiful eyes in surprise. He smiled in delight as if Aradus were an old friend. "Centurion, do enter. How long it has been since I last beheld your . . . face?"

"Sir, I—" Aradus broke in hurriedly.

"Goodness, just arrived and champing at the bit to be of service." He swung a leg to the floor and leaned back against the side curve of the low couch. His lazy stance belied his active mind.

"Sir, as I entered the southeastern gate just now a large crowd of people led by a Jew named Jesus was advancing on the Temple. They were relatively peaceful, but they were proclaiming Him as some sort of leader."

"Jesus, was it? Well to be sure, the high priest and his cronies won't like that a bit. There's some sort of power struggle there, though I don't pretend to understand it. Take a couple of men over to the Temple. You can get more men from the Antonia Towers if there's any trouble. I don't think this is anything more than some religious differences, but it won't hurt to be careful."

"Yes, sir."

"Oh, and Aradus . . ."

"Yes, sir."

"Come back this evening. You and I have a lot of catching up to do."

"Yes, sir."

Aradus rounded up a couple of burly soldiers and rode with them across the city to the Temple.

More than half a century earlier, Herod the Great had decided to build a temple that would surpass the one built by Solomon, which had been destroyed by the Babylonians. Ironically, he had used Roman engineers to settle technical problems in the building.

It had been a colossal achievement. Herod had not only built the new temple on the old site but had taken that site and turned it into a mount. The foundation was massive. It was more than two hundred feet above ground in some locations.

The Temple overpowered the city to the south, west, and east. But on the north side, the Fortress Antonia rose over the Temple, a silent testimony of Roman dominion. It was always occupied by troops, and these troops made themselves especially conspicuous at feast times.

The Roman troops were meant to quell an open rebellion. They would not interfere with the Temple unless absolutely necessary. The Temple had its own set of Jewish guards to keep the peace and to make sure no Gentile went past the allowed areas.

Enclosing the hilltop was a colonnade forty-five feet wide, made up of tall, graceful columns of white marble. Within there was the Court of the Gentiles, which Aradus and his men could have entered, but he felt this would be unnecessarily provocative if Jesus and His people had just come to worship.

They rode about the colonnade looking for any signs of disturbance from within the great Temple. From time to time Aradus could catch glimpses of Jesus with a group of men. They seemed to be doing only some harmless sightseeing. The men would often point out some carving or feature while Jesus would look mildly interested.

After an hour or two Jesus and His men left the Temple, going out the Hulda Gate. Aradus instructed one of his men to follow at a distance to see where they were headed. Before the man could proceed, everyone's attention was arrested by a high-pitched shout from the crowd. There was a blur of motion, and Aradus suddenly felt a viselike grip around his right ankle.

Instantly, the two Roman soldiers had drawn their swords and made a tight protective circle around Aradus. He looked down in confusion at his right stirrup, only to see the smiling face of Guni. The boy was laughing and talking rapidly as he pulled on the Roman's leg, oblivious to the two swords pointing at him.

Aradus nearly smiled a welcome, then his soldier's instincts told him Guni's voice was the only one he heard. Anywhere. Aradus looked up to see a vast sea of Jewish faces staring at him and his men. Even Jesus and His men had stopped to look at the sight of one little Jewish boy surrounded by soldiers with drawn swords.

Aradus gave what he hoped was a charming smile, then hissed between clenched teeth, "Fools! Put those swords away! Do you want this mob to think we'd kill a child at the foot of the Temple during Passover? There wouldn't be enough of us left to ship home!"

Wide-eyed the men looked over their shoulders and blanched as they saw the silent crowd. They quickly put up their swords.

"Guni, let go of my leg. Guni, I can't feel my foot." Aradus tried to break through the boy's fountain of talk. "Guni, these people think you're begging for your life. Guni, be quiet!" Aradus finally roared.

Guni was quiet.

But only for a moment. He stared at Aradus with wild eyes, then incredibly began to tug on his horse's reins. "But you must come! Jesus is right over there! Don't you see Him! I saw you, and I couldn't believe it. Then I saw Jesus. It must be God's will. He can heal your face now!" Guni shouted in a breathless rush as he pulled the reins.

Aradus felt an unaccustomed heat spread across his face as he blushed for the first time in twenty years. He knew he was the focal point of hundreds of hostile eyes. This was not the time to be discussing his face! "Guni, stop that! The horse might step on you! Guni!"

Aradus was afraid to dismount for fear the horse might

go forward onto the tugging child. He reached for the boy, but Guni managed to evade his long arms.

"Jesus!" Guni began to shout. "Jesus! Please come here!"

"No!" Aradus whispered hoarsely. "No! Be quiet!"

The silent crowd began to laugh now as the great centurion was harassed by the little Jewish child. Aradus made a final lunge for Guni, only to miss him again. He nearly came unseated in the effort. This provoked a great howl of laughter from all those around.

Furious, Aradus barked at his men. "Hold this horse while I dismount."

With the horse secured, Aradus fairly leaped from the saddle, determined to spank Guni, even if the mob stoned him to death.

Such was his haste that he nearly knocked into a man as he landed on the ground. It was Jesus. Aradus found himself staring into a pair of large brown eyes, a pair of very amused eyes.

Aradus was speechless. But it didn't matter, as Guni rushed to fill in the breach. "Here he is! Here he is!" Guni was fairly dancing around the two men. "Go on, Jesus. You just go on and heal him!"

An earthquake would be nice or perhaps a bolt of lightning could burn me into the ground just now, Aradus thought calmly to himself. He was reconciled to this public humiliation for the moment, knowing how bitterly he would regret it later.

"Guni," Jesus said gently. "Perhaps we can discuss this somewhere else?"

Guni was suddenly quiet as he looked around for the first time at the vast audience he had acquired. He nodded solemnly.

Jesus led Aradus and his men out the Hulda Gate to a

small, secluded spot.

So now I have only my guards and Jesus' twelve men to shame me, Aradus thought to himself.

"Now, Guni, why don't you explain yourself?" Jesus said in a quiet, deep voice.

Guni took a great gulp of air and proceeded, "This man looks really ugly!"

The guards studied the ground.

"I mean, he's ugly, but not really ugly. He was hurt badly, so he looks ugly, but You can make him look good again!" Guni declared in a burst.

There was a great silence. Aradus folded his arms across his chest and looked at Jesus defiantly.

Jesus only smiled, then bent down to whisper to the boy. Guni began to look sadder and sadder as Jesus continued to speak. Finally, a long tear escaped and made its way down his face. He looked the very picture of sorrow. It softened Aradus.

Jesus straightened and walked to Aradus. "The boy must care about you very much."

It was not what Aradus had expected. "I don't see why," he said gruffly.

"He never meant to embarrass you; he only wanted to help. To see that you were healed of your wounds."

Aradus looked at Jesus. He was a very plain man. He wouldn't have noticed Him more than any of the other Jews in Palestine. His eyes were kind, though. Kindness irritated Aradus. He took it as another form of pity. Would even the Jews pity him now? "Well!" he ground out harshly. "Go on then, magic man! Let's see what You can do." He undid the straps of his helmet and threw it to the ground. "Men made this face; maybe a man can fix it!" he shouted as he thrust his face forward.

Jesus never flinched but only looked at him sadly. "God made that face, and God can heal it, if you want to be healed. I'm not sure that you do."

Aradus turned away. He regretted his lack of control. With the last of his dignity he stooped and picked up his helmet. He laid a hand on Guni's shoulder, who was sobbing as if his heart would break. "Don't, Guni. You meant well." Aradus looked back at Jesus. "Do You think it's right to get such hope up in little children?" he asked angrily.

"Yes. Yes, I do," Jesus answered calmly.

Aradus shook his head in disgust and turned back to the city. His men followed for a while, then on a signal from him, one broke off and quietly followed after Jesus.

The man soon came back, saying Jesus and His men had left the city and gone toward Bethany. Mystified, Aradus returned across the bridge that connected the Temple with the western part of the city.

It had grown dark when Aradus reached the legate's quarters. He was relieved to see the man had lit only two braziers and was not going to repeat his former festival of lights.

"Well, centurion, what nefarious doings did you observe at the Temple?" Livius asked with his usual cheerfulness.

"It was strange, sir. After such an entry, the man left quietly for Bethany," Aradus said simply. He had no intention of recounting to Livius the full details of his personal encounter with Jesus. The legate would only find some way of using his latest humiliation as a weapon against him.

"He bears watching, I'll grant you. But with the fortress breathing down on the Temple as it does, I don't think He's really trying to lead a revolt against Rome. From what I've heard, He's more interested with some popular movement against the Temple hierarchy. He especially seems to have it out for the Pharisees. We won't need to concern ourselves unless it interferes with the ever-smooth workings of the empire."

"Yes, sir."

Livius picked up a piece of parchment from the table. He looked at it, then glanced up at Aradus. "Now, on to more important business. I received this dispatch from Caesarea last week. Really, Aradus, I don't recall breaking jaws as being part of your assignment there." Livius watched Aradus closely, wondering how far the man could be pushed. "They say your attack was totally unprovoked. Is that true?"

"Yes, sir."

"They say the man had a promising military career that you have now cut down. Is that true?"

"Yes, sir."

"They also say he was a young man, just about the age you were when you suffered your own . . . disfigurement."

"Yes, sir."

Livius arose and paced a few feet about the room, wondering how to make the best use of the situation. It was incredible to think how fortunate he was. He could now destroy this centurion and erase the last link to the accursed shields. Pilate would never know the part he had played in the governor's humiliation.

He rubbed his handsome jaw thoughtfully. It really was too easy. If he brought the centurion down, the whole business would be over. Still, who knew what use the centurion could be at some later date? He had such a hold over him now, there was no telling what he could be forced to do when the need arose. No, he was too valuable an asset just to throw away. Besides, he always relished the thrill of the game, even more than winning.

"The legate in Caesarea left you to my discretion. He felt I would know better than anyone how to deal with your behavior. After careful consideration, I propose to put you on a form of probation. If you are properly . . . compliant with all my orders, we shall forget the whole sorry business. I trust you understand me?"

Feeling like he had just been sold into slavery, Aradus nodded. "Yes, sir."

"Good. Pilate will be arriving tomorrow. I want you to oversee the detail at his residence. I understand he is more than willing to put the business of the shields behind him and reach a conciliatory position with the Jews. It will make all our lives easier," Livius said in a rare moment of candor.

When Aradus left the legate's quarters that night, he went straight to his own bed. Not that he slept. He stared at the ceiling, wondering what else Livius had in store for him.

For the better part of the week, Aradus's duties were light. Pilate seldom had any needs that couldn't be better met by his own guards.

Aradus was hearing things, though, that concerned him. It seemed Jesus had caused quite a tumult in the money-changing area of the Temple. He had incited some sort of riot that had nearly called for the Roman soldiers to quell. That would have been a disaster—to have the pig eaters in the Temple during Passover. He had sworn at the thought. The city would have been razed before the revolt was over.

Fortunately, things had quieted down on their own. He had heard snatches that indicated the high priests were actively looking for ways to rid themselves of Jesus and His followers. Aradus conceded that it was probably for the best.

CHAPTER SEVENTEEN

*E*arly in the morning toward the end of the Passover week, Aradus was awakened by a loud rumbling of voices east of the barracks. Hurriedly dressing, he left his quarters and proceeded towards Pilate's villa. He saw a large crowd assembled in the courtyard.

At first Aradus feared revolt had finally come, but then he saw Livius standing in a doorway. The legate was the picture of calm, leaning against the threshold with a sardonic smile on his lips.

Hurrying through the crowd, Aradus approached Livius and saluted. "Sir! What is all this?"

"Steady, centurion. The Jews are just doing a little housecleaning. Look there," Livius pointed to the heart of the crowd, where a man held by two soldiers stood bound.

"It's Jesus!" Aradas said with surprise.

"Yes, He finally went too far. The whole Jewish hierarchy has been raking Him over the coals all night, trying to come up with something to charge Him with. They settled on blasphemy, but I warrant you, they'll come up with something stronger to get Pilate to crucify Him.

"Notice, Aradus, how far back these Jews are keeping." Livius's voice was thick with amusement. "They don't want to be defiled by us pig eaters this close to Passover. Pilate has even consented to come out and meet them in the courtyard." Lowering his voice, he added, "The governor has become remarkably agreeable of late."

"Herod is here for the Passover; why not send Jesus to him?"

"Herod can't crucify. Pilate can."

Aradus looked over at the man standing so calmly amid the yelling crowd. "Sir, He had a great following. Where are they now?"

"Where most followers go when things get tough. Nursing their wounds, waiting for another leader who won't ask too much of them."

A clatter of footsteps was heard from within, so Livius smoothly stepped aside, suddenly looking the picture of efficient alertness.

Pilate came through the doorway, trailed by his adjutant and two secretaries. At a nod from Livius, the two Roman officers flanked the trio and went forward to meet the Jews.

Pilate had dressed carefully for this confrontation. His white tunic was covered by an intricately carved leather breastplate. On his head he wore a highly polished plumed helmet. A long scarlet cape flowed from his shoulders, down his back and to the ground.

Annas and Caiaphas were both there, making sure to stay a good ten feet away from Pilate and the other Romans. As soon as Pilate approached, the crowd began to scream accusations about Jesus.

"This fellow perverts the nation!"

"He wants to be king!"

"He forbids tribute to Caesar!"

All the Jews were yelling except for the high priest and his father-in-law. They looked steadily at Pilate. They wanted to make sure he got the point of how disruptive this Jesus was to the peace of Judea.

Pilate became irritated. He thought he would be conferring with the Temple vanguard, not harangued by the rabble. His pride had taken a severe beating in the last few months. Despite his desire to appease his superiors, he was not going to be pushed around by these Jews. He held a long arm up for silence. The crowd immediately stilled, sure the death sentence was coming.

He took a step towards Jesus, and the Jews instinctively moved back a pace. "Are You the king of the Jews?" Pilate asked sarcastically.

Jesus did not answer immediately, but swept Pilate's person with a piercing look. "You say it," He answered calmly.

Pilate squared his shoulders and looked over the crowd. They had screamed at him; they had retreated before him as if he were a leper. No, he was not disposed to do them any favors this day.

"I find no fault in Him," Pilate announced imperiously.

Bedlam broke loose. Even old Annas began to shriek like a washerwoman. "He stirs up all of Jewry, from Galilee to Jerusalem!"

Pilate held up his arm again. "Galilee? Is He from Galilee?" he asked.

"Yes, why?"

"Herod is the tetrarch of that jurisdiction." Pilate turned to Livius. "Legate, have Him sent to Herod!"

With a magestic sweep of his cape, Pilate turned and went back to the villa, leaving Aradus and Livius to deal with the howling mob. Livius made eye contact with

Caiaphas, then made an all but undetectable shrug. A small quartet of soldiers appeared for the escort, changing places with the Temple guards.

"Aradus," Livius called. "I'll let you lead this parade." Walking over to the centurion he spoke softly, staring at Caiaphas all the while. "Plan on making a day of it. Pilate thinks he's won a point here. Herod Antipas just happens to be one of the leaders who wrote that petition about the shields to Caesar. So the governor thinks he's going to give him a nasty little present with this Jesus."

Aradus wondered if he would ever hear the end of those infernal shields.

"But this whole business is being managed by far craftier men than Pilate," Livius continued. "Mark me, before it's over Pilate will do their bidding."

Aradus stared into the man's golden eyes, wondering at the world of deceit that lay behind them. He wondered just how closely Livius worked with the Temple priests.

After a few more instructions, Aradus set off with the group for Herod's residence.

Herod Antipas came to Jerusalem every year for the three great feasts. Because the Romans had taken over his father's immense palace, he stayed at the older and less imposing Hasmonean Palace. It was located on the edge of the Valley of the Cheesemakers straight across from the Temple.

Herod came from Idumaean stock, a people who had been compelled to adopt Judaism, so few people looked upon him as a real Jew. Still, King Herod liked to adopt all the trimmings of the Jewish religion when it suited his purpose.

As he had every intention of celebrating the Passover, Herod kept Aradus and his men waiting in the courtyard. He sent word that he would have Jesus brought into his palace by the Temple guards, then after examination, he would be brought out again.

Aradus was disgusted at having to turn his charge over to the Temple guards, but he could see no help for it. It was standard procedure.

Aradus turned to speak to his men and saw that Jesus was watching him. His eyes were not remarkable in themselves, but they seemed now to be filled with a great intensity. Aradus found himself drawn to them. He wondered at such eyes set in that plain face.

Something tugged for a moment at Aradus's memory—yes, that passage from Isaiah. How did it go? "He has no form or comeliness . . . there is no beauty that we should desire Him." Strange that he should think of that now.

Aradus nodded at the men and the Temple guards. They grabbed Jesus roughly, nearly dragging Him into the palace. The mob of Jews followed hard after.

Aradus and his men had nothing to do but wait. Like most men of his age and class, Aradus had a wonderfully cultivated memory. He usually used moments of enforced waiting to drag up bits of literature or poetry. As he stood standing in the palace courtyard he began to recall the Book of Isaiah. Certain verses seemed very appropriate to the present circumstances.

"He is despised and rejected of men." Well, that's true enough, Aradus thought. "We hid, as it were, our faces from Him." Where were all of Jesus' followers?

Aradus blinked. What was he doing? Was he attributing the role of Isaiah's redeemer to Jesus? What errant nonsense. The Jews said their Messiah would be a military king. This man had no army. Whatever followers He had were already dispersed.

Aradus's thoughts were interrupted by a snort of amusement from one of his men. Aradus turned towards him as the man muttered to another soldier. "Yes?" Aradus asked coldly.

The man look uncomfortable but spoke out, "I was just saying how happy this is going to make Herod, sir."

"How's that?" Aradus asked surprised.

"Well, sir, it's said that Herod's been just wild to meet Jesus. Herod loves magicians and all that sort of thing. He thinks this Jew is a sorcerer."

Aradus nodded, getting the joke. Old Pilate was being thwarted at every turn.

After an hour's wait, the Romans could hear a loud buzzing of voices. The Jews were coming out.

Aradus was greatly surprised at Jesus' altered appearance. Looking disheveled, He wore an expensive purple robe. A gruesome crown of long, hard thorns was on His head. It had not been gently placed there either, but jammed on with such force that blood was streaming down the man's face and into His eyes. The man was still very calm, though the constant dipping of His head showed what pain He was suffering.

Stepping forward, Aradus demanded, "What is all this?"

"This is the king of the Jews!" someone jeered

Puzzled, Aradus turned to Caiaphas who had just joined the group. "I don't understand."

"You don't have to, soldier. Just bring the man along. I have a message for your governor from Herod."

While certainly not gentle, Aradus's men treated Jesus in a more professional manner. They allowed Him to walk under His own power. It occurred to Aradus that it had probably been hours since the man had last sat down. He must be exhausted.

Sympathy was not part of the centurion's nature, but he did feel a certain affinity for the man. He knew what it was like to have his own people turn on him.

In a relatively short time they were back at Pilate's villa, waiting for him to come out. He came out in a rage, followed this time only by Livius and a rather harassed-looking secretary.

Aradus stepped forward and saluted.

Glaring at him, Pilate demanded, "What are you doing back here? Why have you brought this man with you?"

Before Aradus could speak, Caiaphas came forward a pace and began talking smoothly. "King Herod sends greetings, Governor. He respectfully reminds you that the worst of this man's crimes were done in Jerusalem. He defers to Roman jurisdiction."

Pilate looked as if he'd been struck. A servant came up from the villa, bowed low, and handed Pilate a note.

Pilate glanced at it, then threw it in disgust to the ground. "So even my wife is having nightmares about the man." He turned to the servant, "Tell her I will deal with the man as I see fit!"

Pilate turned back to Jesus. He crossed his arms across his leather breastplate and bent his head forward in deep thought. "Did You say it was unlawful to pay tribute?" Pilate asked.

Jesus regarded him but said nothing.

Pilate waited a full minute, then continued, "Have You claimed to be the Jews' king?"

Jesus was silent.

"Man, don't You know I can have You crucified?" Pilate was beside himself with frustration.

"You could have no power at all against Me, unless it had been given you from above. Therefore the one who delivered

Me to you has the greater sin," Jesus replied in calm, measured tones.

Pilate turned to the chief priests, his finger pointing at Caiaphas's long nose. "Look you, I've examined Him. There's nothing to warrant crucifixion. I'll scourge Him if that will please you, but I have no reason for detaining Him. He'll be the prisoner we release at every feast."

"No!" the crowd roared as one.

"But I thought He was your king!" Pilate yelled angrily.

"We have no king but Caesar!" Annas called out vehemently, striking his cane on the pavement.

Pilate blinked. That was something he should have said.

"Crucify Him!" a man yelled.

Pilate paced like a caged animal. The whole business was getting out of control, out of his control. "Why?" Pilate yelled, though he could hardly be heard above the din.

"Crucify Him, crucify Him," the Jews bellowed over and over in a deadly chant.

Aradus sent one of the soldiers for reinforcements, not sure if the crowd would riot. Livius stood near, his face carefully neutral. The secretary, a small thin man, stayed close to the officers, hoping they would afford some protection if things got ugly.

Pilate stood alone a few feet away. Forced again to do what he least wanted, he held up his hands for silence. The crowd, en masse, became still. Turning to Aradus, he said slowly, "Two others were to be crucified today. Scourge this one, then crucify Him with the others."

"And He made his grave with the wicked," Aradus murmured with a sense of growing wonder.

"What's that, Centurion?" Livius asked sharply.

Aradus didn't look at Livius but continued to stare at Jesus as he answered, "I was just recalling something I'd read. It seemed very . . . appropriate . . . to the present circumstances."

The legate gave a snort of derision, then turned to watch as the little secretary tried to get Pilate's attention. "Sir," the man asked timidly, "what shall I write on the titulus for His cross?"

The titulus was a placard that Roman custom demanded be put on the top of each cross. It explained who was being crucified and why. It would be carried in front of the victim on the march to Golgotha, then nailed to the top of the cross.

Pilate thought for a moment, then an evil grin worked its way across his sour face. "Jesus of Nazareth, King of the Jews."

Instantly, a howl of protest rose up from the priests, but Pilate laughed and returned to the villa.

CHAPTER EIGHTEEN

*T*he scourging would take place at the barracks. At least, Aradus thought, these screaming Jews won't follow us there.

Aradus had been present at many scourgings in his career. He was quite hardened to the cursing and screaming as the prisoner was forced to his knees and lashed to the post.

It was different today. With amazement, Aradus watched as Jesus knelt down as soon as He approached the post. He offered no resistance at all.

Aradus had heard the claims concerning Jesus. He was a miraculous healer, the Jewish deliverer. He'd even heard the myth that He was God Himself. Aradus had dismissed it as vain words.

The sight of Jesus quietly kneeling at the post, waiting for the lashing to begin, affected him more than anything he could have heard.

"He was afflicted, yet He opened not His mouth; He was led as a lamb to the slaughter, and as a sheep before its shearers is dumb, so He opened not his mouth." Aradus had spoken so softly he'd been sure no one could hear him. Yet as he gazed at Jesus' face he knew he was wrong. Jesus had heard.

Aradus rubbed his jaw as a growing sense of confusion filled him. Who was this man? Worse yet, what was this man?

A soldier, famous for his strong right arm, came forward carrying the dreaded whip reserved especially for scourgings. This whip had a thick leather cord that broke into nine branches. Each branch held a piece of bone or metal.

Aradus couldn't believe he was feeling this way. He must have given this order fifty times. If only the man would scream. If only He would stop staring at him.

"Sir?" the soldier with the whip asked uncertainly.

Aradus glared at him, irritated. "Do it then," he ordered.

The man took a step backward, pulling his powerful arm back and up. With all of his strength, he brought the whip down on Jesus' back, dragging the nine jagged ends from His shoulders to His waist.

Jesus arched His back in agony, straining at the ropes that held His arms. He gasped in a great explosion of breath, but He didn't scream.

The soldier stopped amazed. They always screamed.

"Get on with it, man!" Aradus yelled, guilt eating at him. "Thirty-eight more."

Embarrassed, the man put everything he had into the lashing. Over and over he brought the whip down, over and over he dragged the ends through the skin, until the skin was gone and only blood and muscle was left. Still the man didn't scream.

He was gasping, sucking air into His lungs as the pain racked Him. His eyes were not as focused as before, but they never left Aradus's face. Those eyes would haunt him to the end of his days.

The soldiers stole glances at each other. They had never seen a man who wouldn't scream, yell, or curse during the dreaded scourging.

Finally it was over. The thirty-nine lashes were given. Jesus held to the post for support, rather than lying senseless in the dirt as so many did.

Aradus called for the other two prisoners to be sent for, then ordered a group of soldiers to go to Golgotha to put a trio of posts in place. The prisoners would carry their own crossbars to the site.

Nodding towards Jesus, Aradus said quietly, "Help Him up."

Two soldiers untied Him and set Him on His feet. He weaved uncertainly but didn't fall. Looking at the raw meat that used to be Jesus' back, Aradus wondered how He would ever manage to carry the heavy crossbar.

The other prisoners were soon brought and the crossbars placed on all three of their shoulders. Jesus had the most trouble staying upright. As they left the barracks gate, they were met by an immense host of people. It seemed all of Jerusalem was waiting outside of the barracks to follow them down to Golgotha.

It was a short walk to the crucifixion site, but Aradus stayed alert in case some followers of Jesus finally mustered up enough courage to help Him escape. He almost hoped that they would. He led the whole procession, so he couldn't see Jesus struggling behind him. He had an uncanny feeling, though, that the man was still watching him.

Aradus suddenly heard a loud thud. Turning he saw that Jesus had fallen under the weight of the heavy wood. He motioned to a finely dressed man standing in the crowd. The man looked disgusted when he realized what Aradus wanted. But without comment, the man lifted the heavy crossbar to his own shoulders and began to walk with the processional.

Without thinking, Aradus reached down and helped Jesus to His feet. He had never touched a prisoner since he had become a centurion. Yet it seemed so natural now. Jesus placed His hand on Aradus's shoulder as He tried to steady Himself. Aradus was forced to look Jesus in the face. "I don't want to do this," Aradus said softly in his own tongue.

Jesus nodded as if He understood.

They made it to Golgotha without incident. Aradus was almost saddened by the thought that no one seemed to care about Jesus enough to protest, even to hurl an epithet of hate at the Romans. What had happened to all His disciples? He had never seen a man so alone.

"He was taken from prison and from judgment, and who will declare His generation?" Aradus wondered how Jesus could fulfill so many of Isaiah's prophecies concerning a redeemer. There were so many coincidences. What if . . . what if they weren't coincidences? He almost gasped as he suddenly realized he didn't want them to be coincidences. He really wanted this man to be the Redeemer. Was he losing his mind? Even if Jesus was the Redeemer He wouldn't redeem him, a pig-eating Roman. Shaking his head, Aradus turned to the work at hand.

Aradus and his soldiers were skilled at crucifixions. With the usual Roman efficiency, they drove the heavy metal spikes through hard bone and soft wood.

They were not bothered by the mad shrieking of the two other prisoners; they had long been used to that. It was the steadfast silence of Jesus that unnerved them.

Once fastened to their posts, the crucified men made a grisly tableau in the midday sun. After an hour the crowd thinned somewhat. Aradus noticed for the first time that the sky was becoming very dark and a great wind was working up thick cumulus clouds. He wondered what sort of storm could come up so quickly.

There were a few Jews there, some were weeping openly. He couldn't explain it to himself, but he hoped they were crying for Jesus.

Aradus walked over to where a group of his men were gathered. As he drew close, he saw they were playing one of their simple gambling games so popular with all the soldiers.

Upon closer inspection, he saw they were gambling for the cloak Jesus had worn earlier in the day. It was a common practice for the soldiers guarding a crucifixion to do this. Aradus had done it himself many times. Still today, it revolted him in a way he couldn't understand. For the first time in his life, he had to admit that Jesus, this Jew, had behaved better than his own people.

The soldiers looked up at Aradus's surly face and wondered what he was mad about now.

"Let's put an end to this. You there," he said pointing to one of them. "Take the cudgel and break their legs. The sooner they're dead, the sooner we can go."

The man hurried to do as he was bid. Aradus carefully kept his back to the crosses and stared at the men gambling as if it were the most interesting sight in the world.

Piercing screams rent the air as club smashed into bone. Aradus sighed with relief; this strange man was gone.

The soldier came back to report. "All dead, sir. Only had to break two set of legs, though. The one in the middle was already dead."

"What?" Aradus turned to face the crosses.

He was dead. It wasn't possible. No one had ever died that quickly. Aradus stared at the limp body sagging on the cross. Blood and water flowed freely from the fresh wound the soldier had made with a spear to verify His death.

Relief mingled with the Roman's surprise. At least this travesty is over, he told himself. Yet how could He have died so soon?

His thoughts were suddenly interrupted by the sound of shouts from within the city walls. He scarcely had time to react before the shouts were followed by a long, low rumbling. The rumbling noise quickly grew to such an unbearable pitch that Aradus and everyone around him were forced to cover their ears for the pain. Yet their ears were hardly covered when the earth buckled and pitched them to the ground.

Aradus had experienced earthquakes before. But nothing could compare to this. He tried to stretch himself flat on the ground, only to be tossed as if he were a leaf in the wind. He scrambled for the base of the cross, hoping to hold on to anything solid. Just as his fingers touched the wood, the earth gave an incredible heave and flipped him over onto his back.

He found himself staring up into the bloody face of Jesus. It was too much. He threw his shaking arms across his eyes to blot out the sight. As the ground continued its awful vibrations, he realized with horror that the cross could easily topple and fall across him.

"No!" he moaned to himself. "No!" he screamed aloud.

Suddenly the earthquake stopped. An unearthly quiet followed. The stillness was so complete that his ears almost ached as much from the silence as they had from the noise.

Slowly Aradus uncovered his eyes. The battered body still loomed over him, but now he looked at Jesus in wonder.

Something had broken within the hardened soldier. He was lying prostrate at the foot of the cross, and he was totally unmindful of those around him.

With the greatest care, Aradus got to his feet. He moved with deliberation, as if the world was suddenly made of glass. His eyes never left the face that hung above him.

"Truly," he announced, "this was the Son of God!"

CHAPTER NINETEEN

Aradus made his way into the city, stumbling like a drunkard. He was bareheaded, not remembering when he had removed his helmet or even where it was. He was too absorbed with his own maelstrom of thoughts and emotions. He made his way mechanically to his own barracks, his own room. People jostled him, his men asked him questions, but he didn't notice.

After finally reaching his own small chamber, he shut the door and sat down upon his bed. He rested his elbows upon his knees, cradling his head in his hands.

What did it all mean? What could it all mean? he asked himself. Is there a God? Could you kill God on a man-made cross? But they hadn't really killed Him, Aradus knew. Yes, they had crucified Him. He'd given the command with his own wretched mouth. Still, no one died that fast, at least not a young, healthy man like Jesus.

His frenzied mind raced, trying to make sense of it all. Just before He died Jesus had cried out, "It is finished." Aradus hadn't really realized it at the time, but shortly after

149

that a soldier had noticed He had died. It was as if . . . as if Jesus had made the decision. As if He'd allowed Himself to die. No, it wasn't possible.

A small slit high up on the wall was the room's only source of light. Its single shaft of weak light made a slow journey toward Aradus. Yet Aradus sat quietly, his head in his hands. Finally, the tiny sunbeam fell on Aradus. Feeling its warmth, he turned his face to the light. Like a benediction, it rested on his tortured brow. His face cleared for the first time that day. The window was too small for him to see the sun, yet the light showed him it was there. It occurred to him for the first time in his life that, yes, there really could be a God. Even if he couldn't see Him, God could be there. Was that what Jesus had been trying to do? Be a light shining through this dark world?

What if there was a God? What then? Wouldn't he have to do something about it?

He stared into the light for a few moments, then whispered hoarsely. "God, . . . are You . . . are You there?"

He waited, for what he didn't know. An angel didn't appear. The ground didn't quake. The light poured out its little stream from the window and that was all.

It was enough somehow. Aradus knew the sun would soon set and his small chamber would be black with the coming night. But as dark as the night would be, the sun would rise again in the morning.

He stretched out on the thin pallet of his bed. In moments he was asleep. His face, deformed as it was, held the peaceful repose of a little child.

The next morning, the light had hardly made it to the window when a heavy banging sounded on the door. Startled, Aradus sat straight up before he was fully awake.

"Enter," he called groggily.

A small, barefoot boy came in and stood at the foot of the bed. They stared at each other for a moment. Aradus wondered what he wanted, and the boy couldn't remember seeing the man so disheveled.

"Well?" Aradus prompted.

"Oh!" the boy started out of his reverie. "Pilate wants to see you, sir."

In one smooth motion, Aradus swung his feet off the bed and went to the door. Then a thought arrested his movements: I can't present myself to the governor like this. Turning he said, "Boy, get me water to wash with. Bring me some bread too."

He'd noticed he was faint with hunger as soon as he had gained his feet. When had he eaten last?

In a short time he was ready and on his way to Pilate's. The peace of last night had fled. As he made his way, he worried about this summons. Should he have reported in? Had he left Golgotha too soon? Had he been derelict in his duties? The greatest concern was the crucifixion itself. If there was a God, what had he done?

He heard the din of loud voices long before he entered Pilate's courtyard. Upon entering the place he saw a crowd of the chief priests and Pharisees haranguing the governor. What now? he asked himself with exasperation.

"It's not over yet!"

"It could be even worse!"

"They'll lie!"

These were just a few of the loud exclamations shouted at Pilate, before he held his hand up for silence. "I may have two ears, but I can only hear you one at a time," he said waspishly. He half turned, presenting his back to all on the left side of the palace. He looked sourly upon those at his right, fixing his baleful stare upon Caiaphas. He made a limp motion with his hand, indicating the priest should step forward.

"The man's dead. Are you still afraid of Him?" Pilate asked with a sneer.

The priest was too scornful of Pilate to be irritated by him. He carried himself proudly erect, as if he were the governor instead of Pilate. "We are concerned by His zealous followers, who would rebel against Caesar," he returned smoothly. "A concern that you should share."

Pilate stiffened at the rebuke. The priest continued before he could retort. "Sir," he said silkily, "as we have already stated, we remember how that the deceiver said, while He was yet alive, 'After three days I will rise.' Therefore command that the tomb be made secure until the third day, lest His disciples come by night and steal Him away, and say to the people, 'He has risen from the dead!' So the last deception will be worse than the first."

Pilate noticed Aradus standing across the way. He had originally sent for him to discuss the events of yesterday, but he would serve this purpose just as well. Without acknowledging him, Pilate turned again and faced the room.

"You have a guard," he said with disgust. "Go your way; make it as secure as you know how."

He stood and faced Aradus. "Centurion, scout out your finest soldiers. Pick only your fiercest warriors. Then set them to watch over the dead man so He won't escape!"

Pilate's derisive laughter couldn't cover his feeling of helplessness. When had he stopped being in control of this rabble? He felt caught in a flood of events that were sweeping him to disaster.

Confused, Aradus saluted and led the group from the courtyard. Immediately they began to make demands. They told him how many guards were needed, how many shifts to have, what to look out for. Aradus walked in agitated silence until they regained the street. Once clear of the palace gates he whirled to face them. In his own tongue he loudly questioned their sense and their parentage. Then when he was calmer, he addressed them in Greek. "I am a Roman soldier! Roman! I take my orders from Romans not from . . ." He desperately wanted to say murderers, but finished lamely with "Jews." "Now tell me where this grave is so I can post my men," he demanded.

The offended group puffed up and began to complain at his tone, but the chief priest waved them off. He looked hard at Aradus. "This . . . soldier," he said dismissively, "knows his duties. I think we can trust him to do them."

After giving Aradus directions to the tomb the priest turned and began to walk away. As a parting shot, he looked over his shoulder and called to Aradus, "Do your job well, soldier. We must please Caesar."

Aradus returned to the barracks to get the necessary soldiers. He wondered why they were being asked to guard a dead man's tomb. Surely the priests didn't believe Jesus had any followers left, especially followers daring enough to steal His body. Besides, who could be foolish enough to believe any claims of a miraculous resurrection?

Thinking over the events of yesterday, Aradus conceded if anyone could rise from the dead, it would have been this strange man. Aradus sighed deeply. But the man was very, very dead. Whatever good He might have done, whatever hope of a better life for His people He might have brought, had been crucified with Him. Aradus himself had given the orders.

Hope, Aradus had found, was as elusive as peace. He was sure he would never possess either one in this lifetime.

"Ah, Aradus, my ever-present stormcloud." Aradus

turned at the hateful sound of Livius's voice. The legate was coming towards him from across the compound. Aradus stopped, waiting for the man to come up. "It occurs to me, I have never once seen you smile," Livius said pleasantly. "Can you? Or is that another effect of your injuries?"

Aradus only saluted, though he wished he could bring his arm back a little farther and knock the man's head from his shoulders.

"Word has it that you are now in charge of dead men, Aradus. Hardly dignified duty, I'll grant you. Though it might be more important than you suspect." Livius paused for a moment, thinking how to continue. "The Passover week is nearly finished. All the country Jews will be going home soon. It is to everyone's advantage that they leave here knowing beyond a doubt that this Jesus is as dead as old Caesar Augustus. Don't discount His disciples yet. They may not be brave enough to withstand Roman soldiers, but a little grave robbing is certainly not beneath them."

"Yes, sir."

"Keep at least two soldiers posted at all times. We'll need to be especially vigilant the next couple of days. If they do try anything it will most likely be soon."

Aradus was surprised that the usually laconic Livius was so concerned. He wondered what difference such things could make to him. Without meaning to, he telegraphed his thoughts to the ever-observant man.

"Poor Aradus, you just can't look beyond the surface, can you? The empire works very well here; the Temple priests work well with the empire. I, for one, am not going to let anything or anyone upset such a good relationship. If the common people ever truly believed that Jesus rose from the dead, it would ruin everything. They would stop looking toward the priests for guidance—after all the priests had

Him killed. If the priests couldn't rule the people, our job would become three times worse. No, it's important to all of us that that Jew stays in His tomb."

CHAPTER TWENTY

That day and the next Aradus would often walk down to the sepulcher to make sure all was well. It was a small whitewashed tomb set in a garden. It was a very peaceful place, and Aradus had to admit it was pleasant to go there.

It was a very costly tomb, donated by a wealthy man named Joseph. Aradus thought it ironic that Jesus' grave should be worth more than any possessions that He had in life. But then again, what had Isaiah said? He "made His grave with the wicked—but with the rich at His death."

Aradus was badly confused. Jesus had fulfilled so many of Isaiah's prophecies of a redeemer. Yet here He was cold in His grave. The day of the crucifixion, Aradus had been so sure He was the Son of God. Now all he had was doubts. He was beginning to doubt his own sanity.

No Jews were about, as any contact with the tomb would keep them from celebrating the Sabbath. He imagined there might be someone coming at the first of the week, though, to anoint the body.

For now there was only Aradus and the two soldiers posted for the watch. He tried to look official as he examined the seal on the tomb, not that he really thought anyone had tampered with it. No, what he really wanted was just to be there. He wished he could be alone in the little garden, to think things through. He felt an overwhelming need to apologize to the man inside the tomb. Not that He could hear me, Aradus thought bitterly as he left for his day's work.

The first day of the week, after finishing an early morning drill, Aradus left to go down to the sepulcher. As he passed by Livius's quarters, he noticed the door was wide open. Curious, he thought, the wretch usually slept much later.

Aradus made his way out of the city and into the garden. Dew was still on the cypress trees that bordered the place. As Aradus came around the trees he stopped in amazement. The great stone guarding the sepulcher had been rolled away some distance. His men were missing completely.

He couldn't understand it. Running to the tomb's opening he looked within. The body was gone but the graveclothes remained. Why? He looked around for blood or any sign of a struggle, but there was none. What had they done with his men? Grabbing a piece of winding sheet he ran back to the city to sound the alarm.

He had not yet entered the city gate when he saw Livius walking toward him flanked by the two men who should have been watching the tomb.

"Sir!" he called, "what's happened? The body—"

Before he could finish Livius grabbed him roughly by the arm. "Shut up, you fool! They told me I'd find you at the tomb, mooning about," Livius hissed, his usual smoothness gone. "Shut up and come along."

The four marched back to the tomb, Livius never releasing his grip from Aradus's arm.

Upon reaching the tomb, and seeing its barren emptiness, Livius cursed and slammed his hand against the huge stone. "It's empty! It's really empty!"

"Sir, how . . . how could they overpower these men?" Aradus asked looking at the two shamefaced soldiers. "And the men still be unharmed?"

"How indeed?" Livius asked, his voice thick with frustration. "Tell him, men. Tell him what really happened."

The two men looked uncertainly at each other. Then one began to speak. "It was incredible, sir. There was this great white light—"

"No!" Livius roared. "I said, tell him what really happened."

The man flinched as if he had been struck. "Yes, sir. I'm sorry, centurion. We . . . we fell asleep. And while we were asleep, His disciples came and stole the body away."

"What? I don't believe it!" Aradus said emphatically.

"Oh, you'll believe it all right." Livius's tone was dangerous. "You'll believe whatever I tell you to believe."

Aradus stared at the legate. What was he up to now? But Livius had already turned his attention back to the men. "Do you understand now? Do you know what has really happened?"

"Yes, sir!" they answered in unison.

"Go back to the chief priests then. Tell them we understand each other. They'll have something for you. If this should reach Pilate's ears I'm confident I can keep you secure."

Aradus watched it all in growing amazement. The penalty for falling asleep at one's post was death. As important as this business had been to Livius, he should have run these men through himself. But he was paying them off.

"You believe it," Aradus said in quiet wonder.

"Shut up," Livius growled.

"You believe Jesus rose from the dead!"

"Shut up, I said!" Enraged, Livius hauled back and hit Aradus across the face.

Caught off guard, Aradus staggered against the tomb, his face away from the raging legate. When he turned back around, a smile of pure delight transformed his features. "Jesus did rise from the dead," Aradus whispered.

"You idiot! I should kill you and stuff you in that tomb myself!" Livius forced himself to calm down. His survival instincts were fully engaged now. He turned to the two soldiers. "Well? Get going!"

Livius watched the two soldiers go, then turned back to the still smiling Aradus. He was mystified by the usually sullen man's behavior. "What's the matter with you, Aradus? Have you lost your mind?"

Aradus didn't answer him but reverently held up the piece of winding cloth. "He rose from the dead. He is the Son of God," he murmured softly.

"I don't have to offer you money, you know," Livius warned. "I have enough information to destroy you."

Aradus didn't care. He truly didn't care. Livius could see that. He knew he would have to try another tact.

"Aradus, all this religious business. What is that to us? The Jews are split into so many factions you can't keep them straight. It's a series of traps that only a smart man can stay out of. I don't know how they got Jesus' body out of the tomb. But somebody did. Now it's going to take everything we've got to contain the movement that's going to spring from it." Livius paused for a moment, thinking how to proceed. "I know you hate Jerusalem. You've always hated it. I could transfer you to anyplace you'd like to go. What about Rome? I could arrange it."

The slightest hint of desperation was in Livius's voice. It brought Aradus back to his senses. Still smiling he looked at Livius. "Caesarea. I'd like to be transferred there."

CHAPTER TWENTY-ONE

Aradus had two reasons for returning to Caesarea. First, he wanted to tell Cornelius all that he had seen. He also wanted to make atonement for what he had done to Statius. He wasn't sure how he would do that, but he hoped to find a way.

He was not welcomed with open arms. His superiors treated him with contempt, his equals with silence. All except Cornelius. He actually seemed glad to see Aradus. As soon as Aradus arrived, Cornelius went straight to the man's quarters.

Cornelius stood in the doorway at first, not sure of what to say. He coughed slightly, to gain Aradus's attention, for Aradus was engrossed in reading a scroll. With surprise, Cornelius saw that it was the scroll he'd given to Aradus.

Aradus looked up. When he saw that it was Cornelius, he smiled so broadly his whole face was transformed. Cornelius was amazed. "Cornelius! Thank you for coming. I have so much to tell you. So much to apologize for." Aradus rose to his feet, uncertainty stealing away his smile.

"Sit down, Aradus," Cornelius said kindly as he took a chair. "I have the time for anything you'd care to tell me."

Aradus smiled again as he sat down. "Where do I start? I've done so much, seen so much since I last saw you." He paused for a moment before he continued. "I'm not the same . . . at least . . . I hope I'm not the same man you knew."

"Go on."

"I've always said there were no gods, that there couldn't be in such an awful world. But what I wouldn't admit was that I wanted, so desperately, for there to be a God. Not the vain, heartless gods of our legends, but just one, all-powerful God . . . who would care about . . . me," Aradus nearly whispered the last word, not sure of Cornelius's reaction.

"That's nothing to be ashamed of. I want the very same thing."

Aradus nodded, encouraged.

"Well, then I read the scroll you gave me. It seemed to put into words the very thing I had always wanted. A redeemer, a God-man who would make 'intercession for the transgressors.'"

"Exactly how I felt when I read Isaiah," Cornelius agreed.

"Yes, but then I met Him! Jesus fulfilled it all!" Aradus growing excited, stood again. "And, Cornelius, despite what you may have heard, He did rise from the dead! I know it!"

Cornelius looked at him with wonder, wanting to believe him. "You're sure, Aradus? We've received so many strange reports."

"I know it's true. I was there when the legate bought off the guards."

Cornelius lowered his head for a moment, then with tears streaming down his face, he lifted his hands palms upward and began to pray.

Aradus stared at him for a moment then said gently,

"You pray as the Jews do. Why?"

Cornelius smiled as he wiped his tears away. "I have much to tell you too. I worship the God of the Jews, and I follow Him as closely as my military duties will allow."

"Who knows this?" Aradus asked, stunned.

"Only those I can trust."

"Thank you for that trust, but before you tell me anymore, I must confess something to you. I know you will hate me, despise me really, but you must know."

"All right, then."

Agitated, Aradus began to pace the room. He picked up the scroll he had left on the bed and held it to his chest. "I've always followed orders. Always. I suspected that Jesus was different, special. But I wasn't sure. So when I was ordered to have Him . . . crucified, I . . . did as I was told." Aradus was no longer looking at Cornelius, so great was his shame. "Jerusalem isn't like Caesarea. Crucifixion is the only way to keep the populace under control. I've overseen dozens of crucifixions since I was posted there. But this one will haunt me to the day I die."

Cornelius had no words of comfort to offer him. He knew the man's guilt must be overwhelming.

"Aradus, I certainly don't despise you. You did what you were trained to do. I despise an empire that would train men to kill others in the most painful way possible. I despise an empire that kills men whose worst crime is loyalty to their native country."

Aradus nodded and sat down. He had reached the same conclusions about the empire he had once so proudly served. "Is that why you began to believe in the God of the Jews?" he asked.

"Partly. But it wasn't just from my growing dissatisfaction with Rome. Like you, I had always longed for a God I could know, not just read about. I wasn't in Caesarea very long before I realized how close the Jews felt to their God. He was a Father to them in every sense of the word.

"I read everything about the Jews and their God that I could. I talked to as many religious leaders as possible." He smiled ruefully, "Don't think they didn't all run from me at the first!"

"How did you get them to trust you?"

"Time. I learned not to rush anything, but to get their gradual approval. As the years passed they saw I never harassed their people. I'd also give to the support of the Temple. When they finally knew they could trust me, they taught me everything. It was wonderful. I drank it in like a man dying of thirst."

The two men talked on into the night, sharing their own thoughts and experiences about the Jews' God and Redeemer.

In the months that followed, Cornelius began to train Aradus secretly. He taught Aradus to pray and to give alms for the relief of the city's many poor. He also taught Aradus to speak Aramaic so that he could talk to the people he once so despised.

CHAPTER TWENTY-TWO

The years passed slowly, with Aradus constantly being given the worst jobs and lowliest duties. He took each assignment humbly, feeling it was his due.

He had what he had always wanted, though—peace and hope. Peace in this life, and hope for a better life to come. He couldn't imagine there was anything more to ask for.

Ten years passed from the time he had given the orders for Jesus to be scourged and crucified. He had changed in many ways. His black hair had turned an iron gray. The large dent was still in his forehead, but the great scar along his face nearly disappeared when he laughed, which was often.

He had become quite popular with children of all races and with the city's Jewish population. He shared with Cornelius a deep desire to be allowed in the Temple in Jerusalem, though both men knew it would never happen. They contented themselves with observing the Sabbath at Cornelius's house with a handful of other Gentile God-fearers, hoping that God would accept their frequent prayers.

On one morning, as Aradus made his usual round to Cornelius's dwelling, he was met at the door by his friend. The years had hardly touched Cornelius. He was still as strong and straight as ever. His eyes were still as warm and kind.

His eyes were moist that morning as he met Aradus. His face was glowing. He clasped Aradus by the wrists. "Come in, old friend. Come in."

Two of his more faithful servants were in the room, their faces wet with tears.

"What is it, Cornelius?"

"You and I, we've read about angels and visions for years, haven't we? Believed in such things with all our hearts? But always knowing it was for the Jews. Always and always for the Jews."

"Of course. That is how God wants it."

A beautiful smile lit Cornelius's thin lips. He began to sob like a child. "I've had a vision! I was praying, and an angel of God spoke to me!"

Aradus was thunderstruck. "An angel! An angel! What did he want? Did he say anything?"

"Yes! He told me my prayers and alms had gone up as a memorial before God. Then he said I was to send men to Joppa for a man named Simon Peter. He would tell me what to do."

Aradus sat in a chair too overcome for words. That God would send an angel to a Gentile! It was really too wonderful. "Please, Cornelius," he finally said. "May I be one of the men you send?"

Cornelius smiled at the humble request. How much this man had changed! "Of course, how could I not send you?" he answered.

It was quickly arranged that Aradus would leave the next

day with the two servants. Joppa was a short day's journey away, so the trip was easily accomplished.

Joppa was down the coast from Caesarea. It was built on a rocky mound 116 feet high on the edge of the sea. A good stiff breeze blew on the travelers, making their journey pleasant. They had been told to look for the house of Simon, a tanner, with whom the man called Simon Peter was lodging.

After asking directions from a few of the town's residents, they were able to find the place. Within a block their own noses helped them to find the house. Soaking animal skins in lime and acidic juices created a definite, unique odor.

Like most houses in Judea, this one had a small stone staircase attached to the side of the tanner's house that led to the roof. As Aradus and the servants drew near, they saw a Jewish man descending the staircase.

His hair was thin and gray, receding back from his brow. He seemed to be about fifty and looked as if he had spent every day of his life outdoors. He regarded them uncertainly for a moment, then spoke, "I . . . am the one you are looking for. What did you want?"

In a few words, Aradus related the content of Cornelius's marvelous vision.

Peter looked somewhat dazed, but he nodded in agreement. He stared for a moment at Aradus and his uniform. Then smiling gently, he motioned to the doorway. "Well, won't you . . . won't you come in?" he asked.

It would have been hard to say who was more surprised—the Romans who received the invitation or the Jew who gave it. They stayed the night at the tanner's house then set out the next day for Caesarea. Peter was joined by some of his friends who wanted to be a part of this wondrous venture.

After another day's journey they reached Caesarea and the anxious Cornelius. He had gathered together all of his friends and kinsmen who believed in God. Supposing Peter to be another angel or something even greater, he humbly knelt as soon as he saw him.

Peter quickly took him by the arm and gently led him into the house. "I am a man just like you," Peter said, then looked around at all the people gathered there. "You know it is unlawful for a Jew to enter a Gentile's house. But God has told me not to call anyone common or unclean. Now tell me, why have you sent for me?"

Cornelius repeated his vision to him and how God had said Peter would tell him what he needed to do.

With a look of delight Peter spoke to the group, "Truly, God is no respecter of persons."

He then began to speak of all that God had tried to do with Israel and of all that Jesus had done. He spoke of the healings and miracles that he had personally seen Jesus do. The Romans nodded, eagerly drinking it in. He then began to speak of how Jesus was crucified, which caused Aradus to hang his head. Then Peter talked of how Jesus was raised from the dead, which caused Aradus to lift up his head again.

Finally Peter began to speak of the power of the name of Jesus. He explained, "Through His name, whoever believes in Him will receive remission of sins!"

Something incredible began to happen to Aradus as he heard these words. He felt the weight of his sins, and his heart cried out to the Lord for forgiveness. Suddenly, he felt as if he'd been placed in an ocean of warmth, with wave after wave surging though him. There was a whiteness when he closed his eyes that was as bright as the desert sun. He had a sudden desire to shout, to praise God. He couldn't contain it, he just had to shout praises to God. But when he finally burst out, it wasn't in Greek or Aramaic or even Latin. It was a strange language no one else knew.

The other Romans didn't notice him, though. They were too busy having the same experience. Some laughed, some wept, but all expressed uncontainable joy.

The men who had come with Peter were astonished. How was this happening? But they soon forgot their questions as they too were caught up in the sweeping waves of worship.

Peter knew these Gentiles had received an outpouring of the Holy Spirit as real and authentic as any the Jews had received. He basked in the presence of the Spirit, often reaching out to hug one of the Romans.

After a long time of worship, Peter called out joyfully, "Can anyone forbid water, that these should not be baptized, who have received the Holy Spirit just as we have?" Then he commanded them to be baptized in the name of Jesus Christ.

The group began to file out of the house, intent on going down to the seashore for a great mass baptism. It happened that Peter and Aradus were the last to leave the house.

Aradus motioned Peter aside. "This is all so wonderful. But, Peter, I think you should know something about me. Something horrible."

"Yes?"

"I . . . I was the officer who gave the orders for Christ to be crucified."

Peter looked at the man with all the compassion he had. He placed his hand on Aradus's shoulder. "And I was the disciple who denied Him. But you must believe that His forgiveness is available to both of us."

Aradus smiled and followed Peter down the hill to the sea.

171